Sandscreen

By Ian Stuart

Sandscreen

IAN STUART

PUBLISHED FOR THE CRIME CLUB BY

DOUBLEDAY & COMPANY, INC.

GARDEN CITY, NEW YORK

1987

All of the characters in this book
are fictitious, and any resemblance
to actual persons, living or dead,
is purely coincidental.

Library of Congress Cataloging-in-Publication Data

Stuart, Ian.
Sandscreen.

I. Title.
PR6069.T77S36   1987   823'.914   86-16222
ISBN 0-385-23799-5

Sandscreen

2297347

PROLOGUE

Once past the last small town, there was nothing but the desert. Near the road it was level, but in the distance on both sides the sandhills rose a hundred and fifty feet and more, mysterious and slightly menacing in the evening light. It was strange how, if you had never seen the desert, you grew up believing it to be as flat as a plate, a monotonous brown infinity, O'Brien thought. Nor were you prepared for its colours. At midday it could be a dazzling near-white, now it was almost purple. Soon the sun would set in a fiery blaze, and the stars would shine with a brilliance they never possessed at home.

Every few miles he saw a clump of palms marking an oasis and a cluster of single-storeyed mud-brick houses. The landscape must have looked very much like this in biblical times, and long before then, most likely. Only the road was new, a smooth tarmac strip running straight as an arrow as far as he could see across the sand.

A hundred and ninety-five kilometres, they had told him, then he would come to the dunes. The camp was another kilometre beyond them. This was the first time he had come; in the past he had handled his part of the operation from his office or the hotel, waiting there for a message that the goods were ready for shipment, and the unexplained change in the arrangements made him slightly uneasy.

He hadn't seen another vehicle for at least twenty miles. He hoped to God his hired Renault didn't let him down, that would be the end of everything. Perhaps of him. It would almost certainly be hours, possibly well into tomorrow, before anybody came this way. At the time it had seemed slightly ridiculous, but now he was glad he had brought a container of drinking water and some food with him. Only fools played at being heroes in the desert.

He saw the dunes some time before he reached them, a ridge rising seventy or eighty feet above the road, scored into channels and gullies by the wind. He braked, reversed into the space between two shoulders of the sandhills as he had been instructed to do, and switched off the car's lights before looking at his watch. Four minutes to go.

When he got out of the car the air was still hot. He started walking along the road, staying in the shelter of the dunes for as long as he could, although he knew there was nothing for him to fear. The man he was to meet would come to him; all he had to do was drive him back to the city and leave him near the docks. A piece of cake, they would have called it in his young days. A doddle, easy as falling off a log.

After a hundred yards the road began to slope downhill, and just below the crest of the little rise he stopped. He could see the camp now. It was larger than he had expected, long rows of squat concrete buildings arranged in squares and surrounded by a high fence. He thought he could make out coiled barbed wire forming a second barrier. There was an open square in the middle of the camp, and over by the perimeter fence on the other side a larger sandy space. The recreation area, O'Brien supposed. At one corner a tower stood up starkly skeletal against the darkening sky. A water-tower or a lookout post, the light wasn't good enough for him to see which.

Two sentries were on guard at the main entrance, but in the side fence facing him there was another, smaller gate, seemingly without a guard. While he watched, it opened, and a solitary figure emerged. The man was tall, or looked so in the uncertain light, and he was carrying a holdall. There was something furtive in the way he moved, cutting across the sand towards the road, then, when he reached it, hesitating for a second or two before turning right and starting at a fast walk up the slope towards where O'Brien was waiting.

He had covered a hundred yards when a light on the tower was switched on, illuminating the road with its harsh white brilliance. O'Brien hadn't been prepared for a searchlight. It alarmed him. The beam hovered over the man, then moved on. O'Brien watched it coming slowly towards where he was standing, and put a hand up in front of his eyes to shade them. Another second and the wide shaft of light reached him. It seemed to him he could feel it. It was as if it had stripped him naked. He could see nothing against its terrible brilliance, he was pinned to the landscape, as helpless as a butterfly pinned to a board.

Another second, he thought, and it would pass on. Pray God it passed. And it did, groping, probing the dusk by the dunes. O'Brien took his hand away from his eyes and saw the man coming up the road towards him, no more than a hundred yards away.

"Run!" he shouted. "Run, you fool!" It didn't occur to him the man might not understand. Then, as the light swung back, picking O'Brien out standing there, his arms waving, a grotesque, slightly ridiculous figure, a guard on the tower fired.

The sound of the shot was appallingly loud in the still air. Something hit the ground a few feet to O'Brien's right, sending up a spurt of sand. It was followed by a short burst. A bullet pinged off a stone, and another struck the road just behind him.

"Christ!" he breathed. His fear was almost tangible, a sour taste in his mouth and a looseness inside him. He knew now why he had been told to wait in the car.

Almost without thinking, he turned and started running back up the road towards the dunes, zigzagging as he went, trying to escape from the probing beam of the searchlight. He was gasping for breath, his heart pounding.

A few seconds more and he reached the darkness of the cutting. The light couldn't find him there, and there was no more firing. He was dimly aware through his fear and the beating of his heart of the other man coming up behind him, running awkwardly because of the heavy bag he was carrying.

"Get in the car," the man shouted.

What did he think he was going to do? O'Brien thought, his fear making him angry. All he wanted was to get away, as far from the camp as possible, back to the safe anonymity of the city. Running to the car, he clambered in. The man got into the passenger seat, cradling his holdall on his knees. O'Brien started the engine and the Renault lurched forward onto the hard surface of the road.

"What the hell happened?" he demanded as soon as he could speak coherently.

"It was you, you bloody fool," his passenger said. "You were told to stay with the car."

O'Brien turned his head to stare at him. "You're—" he began.

"Never mind what I am," the man told him. "Just put your bloody foot down."

O'Brien obeyed. Ahead of them the road stretched away into the distance.

ONE

On the last evening of his life O'Brien drove west out of the city along the coast road. The sun roof was open and the breeze ruffled his hair. He was thankful it was cooler now, he had never become accustomed to the savage, humid heat of daytime in the city. You had to live out here for months, probably years, to get used to it, and he had never spent more than a few days at a time in Shajiha.

When the road divided he took the right-hand fork, keeping to the coast. Half a mile farther on he turned off onto a strip of tussocky, yellowing grass and stopped the car. It was very quiet up here on the headland, the only sound the gentle roll of surf on the beach forty feet below. Away to his right the city sprawled across its five low hills and the valleys between them, the houses spreading over the slopes like brown ants. It was too far away, and daylight too far gone for him to pick out many individual buildings, but he could just see the domes and minarets of the bigger mosques. Around them the flat roofs huddled together, the houses climbing onto their neighbours' shoulders to peer over them at the rows of similar hovels lining the narrow streets.

Down there men would be smoking their pipes in the doorways and children playing shrilly amid the dust and garbage. Only in the centre, where bulldozers had ripped the heart out of the city's decaying belly, and on the southern outskirts, along the road to the airport, new skyscrapers thrust up towards the darkening sky, their gleaming concrete and glass at once exciting and in some way an affront.

He and Janet might have taken the road out to the airport today, O'Brien thought. By now they would have been home. He realized his feelings for his wife had changed over the last twenty-four hours; he seemed to be seeing her in a different light, as a person, in a way he hadn't for years. He knew it was because he needed her, only she stood between him and his dread of being alone.

It was too late for regrets, what must be must be. He had been out here less than a week, yet already the fatalism of the people seemed to be affecting him. Opening the car door, he got out and walked the few yards to the edge of the cliff. What would Janet think when she knew? he wondered.

In the city there was noise and bustle, the stink of exhaust fumes thick and nauseous in the air, as if the heat were a blanket trapping it and preventing it from escaping. None of that reached him up here. It seemed to him that the city belonged to a different life, one that existed close to and contemporaneous with his own, yet somehow separate from it. He had come from Dhartoum now, but he didn't belong there. Perhaps he didn't belong anywhere any longer, not even in the house in Surrey he and Janet had bought a year ago and which they called home. He was an outcast.

Turning, he looked northwards at the black void where he knew the sea to be. But beyond the pale glow of the breaking surf there was only darkness, except where, far out in the distance, a pinprick of light betrayed the position of a small ship.

A car was coming up the hill from the direction of the city. It was still a long way off, but O'Brien could see the intermittent glare of its headlights as it came along the winding road between the dunes. For a moment longer he stayed where he was, waiting until he could hear the sound of its engine, then he walked back to his own car.

Philip Rayment eyed Grantley and thought, not for the first time, that he rather disliked the Chairman. It did nothing to lessen his feeling that he knew it sprang from fear. Grantley had never overtly threatened him in any way, yet Rayment was rarely quite at his ease with him. Always he was constrained by the worry that he might say the wrong thing, or uncertainty about how Grantley would react. His was the nervousness of the timid in the presence of the forceful, and he resented it.

Also, he suspected that the Chairman despised him a little. Seventy per cent of the time he might seem all sweet reasonableness, but inside he was as hard and tough as steel. Rayment resented, too, the fact that Grantley, although he had started with all the advantages—Eton, Oxford, and the brain to make the most of them—had the soul and instincts of a buccaneer, or a merchant adventurer. He frankly enjoyed the restrained hurly-burly of commerce, and he possessed what people called the common touch. Rayment didn't, and it was a quality he couldn't admire.

There was a small mole on Grantley's right cheek just beside his nose. The mole offended Rayment, like the Chairman's hair, which he wore almost over his collar at the back, and he focused his dislike on it.

"Have you got those names for me, Philip?" Grantley asked.

"Yes, they're here." Rayment handed him a single sheet of paper with four names typed on it, and four slim files. "I can't see why you think we should send anyone," he remarked with the slight petulance that was the farthest his disapproval ever went. "I know somebody should go, but why not leave it to Maxwells? Forster won't like it, he'll think we're interfering, and it's not as if O'Brien was a director."

Grantley knew the Personnel Director had a point. It was the sort of point he would have, he thought contemptuously. Petty. The Chairman would listen patiently to other people's views before making up his own mind, but once he had come to a decision, he disliked having it questioned. After all, he was paid his very considerable salary to shoulder responsibility. Nevertheless his tone was conciliatory when he said, "It'll show them we take an interest—and it'll be good experience for whoever goes."

Rayment gave up; he never pursued any argument long in the face of the Chairman's opposition. "You said you wanted the four to include at least one woman and Lorimer, Borrett's PA," he said.

"That's right." Grantley opened the top file.

"You spoke to him when you went round there." Rayment disliked the Chairman's practice of going walkabout and talking to junior members of the staff. That was the staff managers' job; he himself rarely spoke to any of United's employees except senior people up for promotion, or, thankfully on very rare occasions, employees who had transgressed so badly they were summoned to his office.

"You don't like him," Grantley commented without looking up.

"I don't really know him. He did quite well on his last course, and Borrett says he should be worth considering for something else when he's had more experience."

Grantley smiled to himself. Saying employees would be ready for promotion when they had more experience was Rayment's and Borrett's way of putting them back in the queue. Borrett would prefer it if nobody achieved any sort of seniority until the age of fifty. "But?" he insisted.

"I don't much care for his personality," Rayment answered, as if the words were being drawn out of him against his will. "He's one of those dour Scots, so reserved he's almost uncouth. I can't see him going far until he changes his attitude." Grantley said nothing, and after a moment the Personnel Director added with unaccustomed dryness, "He's hardly the type to smooth feathers out there, or to console a grieving widow."

"Maybe not." Grantley wasn't looking for one of Philip Rayment's chinless wonders, and he wasn't too concerned about a few ruffled feathers in Maxwells' Middle East office; Maxwells would have to learn they were now part of one of the biggest companies in the world, with all that implied. Whoever went, it would be their job to satisfy him that O'Brien's suicide had nothing to do with his work and wouldn't cause the Group any problems, and to help his widow cope with the local formalities and having her husband's body flown home. That was all. Maxwells' head office downstairs would send a letter of condolence and see she received any help and guidance she might need once she was back in the UK. Money, too, if necessary.

"I'll see Lorimer first," he said. He opened the diary on his desk. "Ten o'clock tomorrow morning. See he's told, will you, Philip?"

"What about the others?" Rayment inquired.

"I'll look at them if Lorimer isn't what we want." Philip couldn't be expected to know that the present exercise was only a trial, Grantley thought. Normally he would have agreed with him and not even considered sending anybody; as it was, he was by no means convinced the qualities Rayment so deprecated would rule Lorimer out. Far from it. And they might make him just the man for the real job he had in mind.

"Very well." Rayment was too well mannered to shrug, but his tone implied the same thing.

When he had gone Grantley stood up and went to one of the big windows that occupied most of two walls of his office. Sometimes when he wanted to imbue one of United's bright young people with a sense of his or her responsibility he would take that particular young person to one of those windows and tell him or her to look down at the teeming streets fifteen storeys below. There wasn't a person down there, he would tell them, whose life United didn't touch in some way. Not that many in the world. Its name might not be a household word, but those of the companies it owned were, scores of them. Go into a shop anywhere in the world outside Eastern Europe and parts of Asia and you were likely to find at least one of their products on sale. The Group's activities were so diverse, its interests so far-reaching, even he couldn't remember them all.

Most people meeting Grantley for the first time thought him a big man, but he was no more than five feet ten, and, although he was heavily built, it was the force of his personality, the impression he gave of enormous power only just harnessed, which made him seem bigger. He had worked his way to the top on merit, and few people ever denied it. He was shrewd and far-sighted as well as tough, and when he thought it necessary, he could be hard. Inevitably he had made enemies. But though he enjoyed his position, it was more because of his pride in United and for the challenges it brought than from vanity; he was not a vain man.

One of his principal interests was the structure of United's management. These days, when the major companies were so vast, how could senior management control without stifling initiative? How earn and retain the loyalty of their staffs, when they were so remote?

It was the Group's strategy to appoint people and let them get on with their jobs in their own way, subject to certain guide-lines. Grantley had seen the fruits of too much interference in government. If the people you appointed didn't perform as well as they should, you replaced them, causing as little grief and pain as possible. If he was lucky, a man might be given a second chance; a third one, never.

The difficulty was that nowadays United's interests spread so wide that problems sometimes arose which, for one reason or another, the people on the spot couldn't be expected to handle. There had been the trouble in West Africa last year. A naturally forthright manager, harassed and under pressure, had said too clearly what he thought of one of the country's ministers, and nearly succeeded in having his company thrown out of it. That could have resulted in the whole Group's being blacklisted there. It was not the only incident of its kind. For weeks Grantley had been thinking about appointing an assistant with a roving commission, available to go anywhere at short notice to deal with local difficulties before they blew up into serious problems. Somebody who would be his own man, or woman, answerable only to him. A trouble-shooter, he supposed; Grantley disliked the term. He believed Lorimer might be the right choice, and this business of O'Brien's suicide coming just now provided an opportunity to try him out.

When Graham Lorimer was told the Chairman wanted to see him, his first reaction was amazement. His second was to wonder what he had done. He had seen Grantley only three times in his life; once at a staff dinner; once at a distance at United's sports day; and once, for a conversation that had lasted no more than three minutes, on one of Grantley's walkabouts. Unable to think of anything he had done serious enough to account for the summons, he stopped wondering. It wasn't his nature to meet trouble half-way.

The Chairman's office was large, and walking across it with Grantley waiting, watching them, had undermined the confidence of more than one brash young man. Lorimer was impressed but unworried. It was unlikely the Chairman would waste his time on calling him up here just to give him a rollicking. All the same, he was puzzled.

"Mr. Lorimer, Sir Aidan," Grantley's secretary said.

The Chairman stood up and held out his hand. For a few seconds they studied each other. Grantley saw a man his own height or half an inch taller, dark and strongly built, with a face that was almost rectangular, the jaw was so square, and features rugged rather than distinguished, the eyebrows strongly marked, the mouth wide. He wondered if those features had prejudiced Philip Rayment against Lorimer. Rayment was still fighting, not very determinedly, his bias in favour of public school and Oxbridge men with rather languid good looks. Lorimer had been to an Edinburgh school and a Scottish university. Just as bad, he had a marked Edinburgh accent.

"Sit down, Lorimer," Grantley said. As usual, he came straight to the point. "Do you like your job?"

For some time Lorimer had been thinking in a rather desultory way about looking for something more interesting. Borrett didn't need a PA, he had created the post to bolster his own image of himself, and he was bored. All the same, if the Chairman meant they were sacking him, he wouldn't take it lying down. He did his job well.

"I like it all right," he replied. "It's not very demanding."

"No, I don't suppose it is," Grantley agreed.

"I'd rather have something I could get my teeth into more."

The Chairman leaned back in his chair and regarded Lorimer steadily. "You think you're capable of doing a more challenging job?" he asked.

"Yes, I do."

Rayment would have considered it boastful, but Grantley understood. Lorimer had asked himself the same question, thought about it, and decided he was.

"What do you know about Maxwells?" he asked.

Lorimer wondered if they were sending him there. If it was to be another glorified coffee boy, they could stick the job, he thought. He tried to remember what he had heard about Maxwells.

"It's a transport and shipping company," he answered. "Mainly in this country, but partly abroad. And it supplies oil and gas fields."

"Is that all?" Grantley wasn't displeased. Lorimer's having never worked for Maxwells, and his knowing little about that company, meant he should be free of preconceived ideas and prejudices. He would probably acquire some as he went along; having talked to him, Grantley was pretty sure he would, but that couldn't be helped.

"United took them over about two years ago," Lorimer said.

"Do you know any of their people?"

"Not really. I've played rugger and golf against them."

The Chairman nodded. "Under its board Maxwells is run by four divisional managers," he said. "The Overseas Manager, O'Brien, committed suicide out in Shajiha last night. He was visiting their Middle East office in Dhartoum, and he gassed himself in his car. It's a tragic business, he had a wife and two children. I want you to go out there. Find out why he did it, and make sure it had nothing to do with his work. I don't want any unpleasant messes crawling out from under the stones, financial, sexual, or anything else. Talk to our consular people, if that'll help. They won't want a scandal either, United does a lot of business in Shajiha. And do what you can to make things easy for Mrs. O'Brien; she was out there with him. Make the arrangements to have his body flown home, and that sort of thing."

Grantley reflected that he had pushed the take-over of Maxwells through against the opposition of some of United's other directors because he believed the company filled a gap in the Group's interests. If it became an embarrassment now, there would be plenty of people who would remember that.

He leaned forward. "Do you want the job?"

"I'd like to know why me," Lorimer answered. "Why not one of Maxwells' own people?"

"You spent some time in that part of the world before you came to United." Grantley smiled sardonically. "And you can be spared." He didn't add that, having read between the lines of Lorimer's reports, and on the basis of his two brief conversations with him, he had decided he was the man for the job. Probably for the other job, too. He just hoped he had sufficient tact and common sense not to antagonize local officialdom in Shajiha. "Use your head," he warned him. "I don't want you treading on any toes out there."

"No, sir." Lorimer knew what the Chairman was thinking.

"Well, what do you say?" Grantley demanded. "I'm sorry, you can't have time to think about it. You'll have to fly out tomorrow. You haven't any ties, have you?"

"No," Lorimer said. Not any longer, he thought. He wondered if a year with VSO working at a remote village in the southern Sudan was the qualification for this job the Chairman evidently considered it to be. But he would go. Even if he and Rosalind hadn't split up, his answer would still have been "Yes." And, to be fair, she would have wanted him to go, there was nothing ungenerous about her. "I'd like to go," he answered.

"Good," Grantley said. "You shouldn't be gone more than two or three days, and unless Mrs. O'Brien wants to stay out there, she can fly back with you. If you go along to Mr. Rayment now, he'll tell you everything you need to know, and Mr. Forster, Maxwells' MD, wants to see you at twelve-thirty. Good luck."

"Thank you," Lorimer said.

They shook hands and he walked towards the door.

"And, Lorimer?"

"Yes, sir?"

"I want to see you as soon as you get back. Give Mrs. Wilkins a ring and she'll fix a time."

"Right, sir," Lorimer said.

As he passed Grantley's secretary sitting at her desk in the outer office, she looked up and smiled. "Good luck, Mr. Lorimer."

"Thank you," he said.

TWO

Rayment's office was on the same floor, at the end of a long, silent corridor with prints of historic warships on its panelled walls. Lorimer supposed the men-of-war were intended to be symbolic of United's roots in the eighteenth-century trade with India.

It was clear the Personnel Director disapproved of his mission. Or perhaps it was only of him. He couldn't care less; Rayment was an anonymous bastard like Borrett. The individual companies' staff managers did the work, he was just a bureaucrat. Their link with head office. The fact that he felt bound to appear helpful now meant the trip was Grantley's idea.

"Their embassy is being very co-operative," he said. "If you go round there as soon as possible, they'll give you a visa. You'll need your passport, of course. You have one, I take it?" His tone suggested he wouldn't be surprised if Lorimer hadn't.

"Yes."

"Thank God for that." Rayment paused. "Do you know where Dr. Hutchinson's surgery is?"

Lorimer nodded. "Yes," he said again. The company doctor had examined him a few months before. Three senior men in their thirties and early forties had died after heart attacks in a period of three months, and somebody had decided that all United's staff above a certain grade and over the age of thirty should have an examination. Lorimer had just qualified on both counts.

"He can see you at three to give you your jabs," Rayment said. "There's a seat booked for you on the BA flight from Heathrow tomorrow morning, and a room at the Excelsior Hotel in Dhartoum. Mrs. O'Brien is staying at the Carlton. The cashier's office will give you your allowance in travellers' cheques; if you want any currency, you'll have to get it at the airport. I'll let Mr. Borrett know what's

happening and that you'll be away for a few days. I think that's
everything."

"Not quite," Lorimer said.

"Oh?" Rayment frowned disapprovingly.

"Just what did O'Brien do in his job, and what was he out there
for?"

"He was in charge of all Maxwells' transport and forwarding business outside the UK. He travelled all over the world. Routine visits."

Checking on the local offices to ensure they were working effi-
ciently, Lorimer thought. Renewing old contacts and establishing
new ones. Seeing that local agents still had the ears of the people who
mattered. As Rayment said, routine.

"There wasn't any special reason why he was in Dhartoum? Nothing was wrong out there?"

"Not that I know of. He'd only been there a few days." Rayment
shifted impatiently. "Is that all?"

"No," Lorimer told him. "I want to see his file."

Rayment looked outraged. "That's out of the question," he said
curtly. "Staff files are confidential; nobody outside this department
and the board sees them."

"I know. But O'Brien's dead, and I'm supposed to make sure he
didn't kill himself because of anything to do with Maxwells. If there
are any skeletons in the cupboard, I'm to see they stay there. That's
it, isn't it? I need to know all I can about him."

Rayment's nostrils seemed to flare as distaste and resentment
chased each other across his narrow features. He reminded himself
that sending Lorimer was the Chairman's idea. For some reason of his
own, Grantley had chosen to interfere in a purely staff matter. He
didn't know why, but there was nothing he could do about it, and he
wouldn't put it past Lorimer to go straight to the Chairman behind
his back if he refused to let him have the file. He was brash and
uncouth enough.

"I'll have it sent down to you," he promised with an ill grace.

Lorimer thanked him. "Did you know him?" he asked.

"Barely. I'd met him once or twice." Rayment stood up to indicate
the interview was ended. "For God's sake, don't cause any trouble out
there. The government's left, of course, but I gather their socialism

owes more to Muhammad than it does to Moscow." He smiled at his own feeble joke. "I hope your trip goes well."

"Thanks," Lorimer said. Everybody seemed anxious to assure him he went with their good wishes, he thought wryly.

When he returned to his office after seeing the doctor, there was a large envelope much sealed with Sellotape on his desk. Besides O'Brien's staff file, with CONFIDENTIAL stamped in large red letters across the cover, it contained a map of Dhartoum with the two hotels, the Excelsior and the Carlton, and Maxwells' office marked on it, a brochure describing that company's business, and a copy of its most recent accounts. Lorimer wasn't sure what they would tell him; he suspected Rayment had told his secretary to put something in with the file and she had included everything about Maxwells she could find.

He opened the file. As he had anticipated, there was nothing in it that told him much he didn't already know about the dead man, apart from his age, his salary, and the dates of his marriage and his children's births. He had left a son of seventeen and a daughter three years younger. Poor kids, Lorimer thought. By now they would know their father was dead.

Fastened to the inside of the cover there was a photograph of O'Brien. It must have been taken some time ago, he looked a good deal less than forty-two, with thick dark wavy hair and full cheeks. It was a rather naive face. Had he changed since then? Had the strains and pressures of his job hollowed those well-fleshed cheeks and lined his features? It was hard to imagine the man in the photograph committing suicide.

Lorimer started to read the sheaf of reports, one a year from the time O'Brien had joined Maxwells when he left school at eighteen to the last a few months ago. The usual stereotyped phrases marked his progress from junior trainee to divisional manager, repeating almost ad nauseam that he had a pleasant personality, was keen and worked hard. Later the phraseology changed: he was an efficient organizer and good at marketing, well liked, establishing good relations with customers. He had taken over his last job from Forster when the latter was appointed General Manager in the changes that followed United's take-over just under two years ago.

Nothing suggested why, a thousand miles from home, O'Brien had got into his car, driven out of the city to a lonely headland, attached a pipe to the exhaust, started the engine and, with the windows closed, sat there waiting for the fumes to kill him. What had driven him to that extremity of fear and despair?

Lorimer closed the file, took it back to the top floor, where he handed it to Rayment's secretary, and went to see Maxwells' managing director.

"This is nice," Rosalind said. She saw Lorimer was surprised and smiled. "I quite like seeing you sometimes, I just don't want to live with you any more. We don't have to go into all that again, do we? Because if you want to, I'm not playing."

"No," Lorimer said.

He was never quite sure why he went on seeing Rosalind. It was a form of masochism, he supposed. She was looking particularly beautiful this evening. There was a glow about her. The highlights in her dark brown hair, her eyes, and the jewels in her ears and on her fingers shining in the light of the little lamp on their table all seemed to have an added brilliance. He didn't flatter himself it was because of him. He wondered if she had found another man and was in love, and was surprised how much the notion disturbed him.

"To what do I owe the honour then?" she inquired, a hint of laughter in her rich contralto voice.

"I'm going to the Middle East tomorrow."

"Permanently, you mean?"

"No, only for a few days. But I thought I'd better let you know in case something happens."

"Your death from snake-bite, say?" The laughter almost broke out.

"I don't think they have snakes in the cities," Lorimer said.

"Don't they? Anyway, it was nice of you to think of telling me. It won't come as such a shock now if I hear you're in gaol out there." Rosalind smiled sweetly.

"It's not exactly a pleasure trip," Lorimer told her, determined not to let her put him off. "One of Maxwells' managers committed suicide yesterday. I'm going out to see to things, and help his widow."

"Oh, I'm sorry." Rosalind sounded contrite. "But honestly, why you, Gray? Don't look so offended. I wouldn't have thought you'd be

their first choice to console a grieving widow, that's all. Who picked
you?"

"The Chairman," Lorimer said.

He had hoped to startle her, and he succeeded. "Sir Aidan?" she
exclaimed. "You aren't serious."

"He sent for me this morning."

"Why?"

Lorimer grinned. "He said I could be spared."

Rosalind ate a little more of her veal cordon bleu. "You are coming
up in the world. Perhaps I should come back to you after all."

Here, over a good meal with a decent wine and Rosalind looking so
lovely, it was an appealing thought, but Lorimer knew that that was
all it was. Nevertheless, life had its compensations. Melissa Forster,
for one.

He had been about to leave the managing director's office when
Forster's secretary rang through to say his daughter was outside wanting to see him.

"Send her in, will you, Sandra," Forster said.

Maxwells' boss was in his late forties, a short, stockily built man
with a round head across which his thin dark hair was brushed flat.
He had shrewd, almost black eyes and a belly that hung over the
waistband of his trousers. All the same, Lorimer's first impression had
been one of restless energy. He knew Forster still played cricket and
tennis, despite his figure. He knew, too, that he had a reputation for
driving himself and his staff hard, but that they liked him. He called
them by their Christian names and was universally known as Jim.
After eighteen months as General Manager with a seat on Maxwells'
board, he had taken over as MD seven months ago, and was now a
director of the Group. Forster had come up fast, on merit.

"We had just about finished, hadn't we?" he asked.

Before Lorimer could answer, the door opened and Melissa entered
the room. "Walked" was too prosaic a word, he thought. Melissa
neither strutted, swayed nor glided, yet somehow she seemed to do all
three. She was a little above average height, slim but delightfully
curved, and very lovely, with long dark hair, a perfect nose and a
delectable mouth. Her eyes, as dark as her father's, were thickly
fringed with long lashes.

"This is my daughter," Forster said. "Melissa, Graham Lorimer."

"Hallo," Melissa said. Her voice was nice too.

"Hallo." Reluctantly, Lorimer turned back to her father. "If that's all, Mr. Forster, I have to go home for my passport and take it to the embassy for a visa before they close."

"Right," Forster agreed. "You get along, Graham."

"Where do you live?" Melissa asked, turning her lovely eyes on Lorimer.

"Southwold Terrace, South Kensington," he told her.

"I'll take you."

"That's all right. Thanks all the same."

"It's no trouble, it's on my way. I only came to bring this." She laid an envelope on her father's desk, said, "They're the prints you wanted," and turned back to Lorimer. "Okay?"

"Yes, thank you," Lorimer said. He saw Forster was smiling.

Melissa waited for him at his flat, and it was her suggestion they have lunch before she took him to the embassy. They went to an Indian restaurant just off Cromwell Road. Lorimer, who had already arranged to have dinner with Rosalind, ate sparingly, but Melissa more than made up for him. Her appetite seemed inexhaustible. Lorimer wondered how she stayed so slim.

"What are you smiling about?" Rosalind wanted to know.

"Was I smiling?"

"I'd say it was more a self-satisfied leer. Is she attractive?"

"Gorgeous. I met her today, and she insisted we had lunch together."

"The uninhibited type."

"Um."

"Meaning you didn't have a chance to find out? Hard luck. Later, then."

Lorimer grinned. "That's not very likely. Her father's Maxwells' Managing Director. I don't suppose I'll see her again."

"You mustn't let little things like that stand in your way," Rosalind said encouragingly. "Especially now you're one of Sir Aidan's chosen few. Where are you going to in the Middle East?"

"Dhartoum." Lorimer replenished their glasses. "I wish people wouldn't keep saying 'Good luck,' as if they think I'll need it."

Rosalind laughed.

THREE

Lorimer had almost forgotten how the climate affected you at first. Stepping out of the air-conditioned plane was like opening the door of a furnace, the heat seemed to hit you like a blow in the face. And the smell, the long-remembered, all-pervasive odour, blending drains with spices. It was a relief to reach the comparatively cool, fresh air inside the terminal building.

Apart from his fellow-passengers, the place was nearly deserted as he joined the queue at the immigration desk. The official, trim in his khaki uniform, was courteous and businesslike. When Lorimer explained the purpose of his visit he asked merely, in excellent English, "How long will you stay?"

"Two or three days, I expect," Lorimer replied.

The official stamped his passport, returned it to him, and held out his hand for the next passenger's.

Lorimer went to reclaim his bag. The customs check proved no more stringent than immigration, and he was thankful that Shajiha's relations with Britain were generally good. Borrett had related with a sort of gleeful satisfaction a long story about the problems he had experienced when he visited some other Middle Eastern countries years before. Picking up his case, he looked for the way out.

A man was standing under a sign TAXIS in Arabic and English over one of the main doors. As Lorimer approached he stepped forward.

"What is your name, please?" he asked politely. He was young, his complexion darker than that of most of the people in the building, but marred by an unsightly scar an inch or so long just below his left eye. It puckered the skin and made it seem as if he were about to wink grotesquely.

"Lorimer," Lorimer told him. Surely the hotel hadn't sent a car to meet him?

"You are not Mr. Smith?"

"No. Sorry."

"Excuse me."

The young man turned and hurried out of the building. Lorimer followed more slowly. Outside, the heat struck him again as he looked round for the taxi rank, the sweat springing out on his forehead and across his back. The first taxi in the line was an elderly, rather battered Peugeot with a fat middle-aged man in a grubby sweat-shirt behind the wheel. Lorimer suspected his piratical appearance was only partly due to his brigand's moustache, and wondered how much haggling would be necessary over the fare.

"The Excelsior Hotel," he said, climbing in with his case. The interior of the cab smelt strongly of herbs, stale cigarette smoke and human bodies.

The driver said nothing, but let in his clutch and drove off with a jerk almost before Lorimer had closed the door, swerving round the bends of the exit road so fast that the Peugeot leaned over dangerously, and out onto the main highway leading to the city. The road was eight lanes wide, lined by modern buildings and twin rows of palms that cast small, dark patches of shade on the asphalt. The taxi sped along, narrowly missing a succession of cyclists on old upright machines, already hampered by their jellabas. Lorimer, having no desire to witness the seemingly inevitable accident, sat back and looked out of the other window.

Thus he didn't see the Mercedes until it was level with the taxi. Even then there was at first no reason for him to take particular notice of it; there appeared to be no speed limit, and the Peugeot wasn't travelling as fast as the noise it was making suggested, while the Mercedes was two lanes away. A man was in the back, and as Lorimer watched he raised something he was holding and pointed it at him through the open window. Lorimer saw with astonishment that it was the barrel of a machine pistol. At the same moment there was a sudden staccato burst of gun-fire. Bullets slammed into the taxi's bodywork, making an ugly metallic sound as they tore through the thin steel.

For a second or two Lorimer was too startled to move. It was absurd to imagine anybody could be shooting at him. His brain refused to accept what he saw. It was a hallucination, a trick of the light. It must be. Then his brain clicked. This was no hallucination, it was real, and he had better do something fast, or he would be dead.

In the fraction of time before he moved, the part of the gunman's face not concealed by his gun was clear to him. Then his muscles accepted his brain's command, and he flung himself to the floor of the taxi. His shoulder slammed the steel carriage of the front passenger seat and he cursed. But the firing had ceased. After a few seconds he raised his head cautiously. The Mercedes was forty or fifty yards ahead, speeding away along the wide, straight road.

As Lorimer hauled himself back onto his seat, the Peugeot swerved to the right, narrowly missing another cyclist and a parked car. The driver corrected the swerve and it started veering in the opposite direction, across the front of a small lorry that had been about to overtake it. The lorry's driver leaned out and screamed abuse.

"What the hell!" Lorimer exclaimed. He was less scared than angry.

Then he saw that the driver was leaning forward across the steering wheel. An ominous dark stain on the left side of his shirt was spreading slowly outwards.

Horns were blaring all round them. Somewhere in the distance Lorimer could hear the wail of a police car's siren. Or perhaps it was an ambulance. The taxi was still travelling at nearly fifty miles an hour and starting another long, sickening swerve to the left. A big Cadillac was overtaking them in the outside lane, the man in the passenger's seat staring at them with a horrified expression on his face. Lorimer saw his mouth opening and shutting, but the words were lost.

The taxi struck the American car a glancing blow just behind the rear wheel. There was a sound of tearing metal and it seemed that the two vehicles were locked together. Then the taxi veered to the right, towards a line of cars parked by the kerb outside an office block. As it did so, the driver slumped lower in his seat.

The Peugeot was a standard saloon, and there was no partition between the front and back seats. Leaning over, Lorimer grasped the wheel. As the driver slumped forward, his foot had pressed harder on the accelerator pedal, and the taxi was already moving faster again. But Lorimer was less worried about that than its erratic course. Any second now it must crash, either into one of the trees beside the road, some unfortunate cyclist, or, most likely of all, another car. Turning the wheel, he corrected the swerve just in time to avoid the parked vehicles.

At least now the Peugeot was going fairly straight. But the speedometer was creeping towards the 100-kilometres-an-hour mark. Not far ahead in the same lane, a large articulated lorry was doing no more than eighty. Leaning farther over, his head pressed against the taxi's roof, Lorimer took his right hand off the steering wheel and groped for the ignition key. Sweat was running down his face and inside his shirt. He could taste it salty on his lips. But although his outstretched fingers just touched the key, he couldn't grip it. With an effort, he managed to lean over another couple of inches. His fingers tightened round the key, turned it, and pulled it out.

It seemed a long time before the Peugeot responded. By now the back of the lorry was only a few yards away. But the clatter of the taxi's engine had died and it was slowing, almost imperceptibly at first, then noticeably. The speedometer fell back. Lorimer saw a space between two parked cars and turned towards it. The front tyres collided gently with the kerb, and the Peugeot stopped, its rear projecting into the road.

Lorimer breathed a sigh of relief. The heat and stench in the taxi were nauseating. The driver was half lying across the front seats, blood oozing through his thin shirt. He must have passed out from shock or loss of blood, but at least he was still breathing. Lorimer opened the door and got out.

A small crowd had already gathered and was growing every second. People gesticulated excitedly and shouted at him in Arabic. He had no idea what the words meant, but clearly they were hostile. Above the clamour he could hear the siren's wail, louder now. The Cadillac had pulled up a little farther on, and two men were getting out of it. They might be able to help.

"Ambulance," he said distinctly. The shouting continued unabated and he raised his voice to make himself heard. "The driver's been shot, he needs to go to hospital."

Nobody seemed to understand. Or, if they did, they took no notice.

It required considerable will-power for Lorimer to turn his back on them and open the driver's door. They surged forward, almost pushing him back into the car.

"Ambulance," he said again forcefully.

But the sight of the unconscious driver only brought louder and even more aggressive calls. It occurred to Lorimer that few sights were more ludicrous, and at the same time more frightening, than a mob bawling incomprehensible threats. He suspected that at any moment words would cease to be enough, and somebody would attack him. God knew what would happen then. Probably the whole mob would join in. He wished he remembered more than a few words of Arabic. None of those he did seemed appropriate now.

Doing his best to ignore the clamour behind him, he concentrated on the stricken driver, feeling for his pulse. It seemed to be steady and reasonably strong. He daren't risk moving him, but it looked as if the bullet had hit his arm, and although the wound was bleeding pretty freely, it probably wasn't dangerous, provided he received attention before long. The driver's eyes opened and he looked up blankly.

Lorimer straightened. The men from the Cadillac were pushing a way through the crowd. They were both middle-aged and well dressed, and he hoped one of them at least could speak English. The wail of the siren had come nearer. Now it died away in a sorrowful moan, and Lorimer saw a pale blue car with red markings drawing up twenty or thirty yards away. Two men in khaki uniforms with peaked caps, guns in holsters at their hips, climbed out of it and walked over. At the sight of them some of the crowd faded away. But at least two dozen remained, jabbering excitedly at the policemen and pointing from Lorimer to the injured driver.

Lorimer didn't like his feeling of helplessness. The men from the Cadillac were speaking forcefully to the policemen; it seemed they had some authority, as the uniformed men listened respectfully and then approached Lorimer. The older of them barked a question at him.

"I'm sorry," he said. "I don't speak Arabic. I'm British."

"You English?" The policeman spoke carefully, with a marked accent.

Lorimer let it pass. This wasn't the time to argue about the distinction between British and English; the man's tone was hardly friendly. "Yes," he agreed.

"Your passport," the younger policeman said.

Lorimer produced it from his pocket and handed it over. The man examined it, then showed it to his colleague before slipping it into his own pocket.

"You're keeping it?" Lorimer asked.

The only reply was a barked command from the older man, who had been examining the driver. Lorimer didn't understand it and said nothing. The man took his gun from its holster and jabbed it at him threateningly.

"What the hell?" Lorimer demanded. He had been restraining his anger long enough. Antagonizing the police might do no good, but at least it would make him feel better.

"Your hands up," the younger policeman told him sharply. His English was better than his colleague's.

Lorimer decided he had better obey. He raised his arms and the older man pushed him against the side of the taxi. He had seen men searched spread-eagled like this in countless films and television programmes; he found the experience infuriating and humiliating. It seemed clear the policemen suspected him of shooting the driver.

The little crowd watched with approval as expert hands searched him. When nothing was found, he was allowed to turn round and relax.

"A Mercedes overtook us," he said. "A man in the back fired at the taxi."

It was clear the men hadn't understood. Only the word "Mercedes" meant anything to them.

"Shot from Mercedes," Lorimer said.

The policemen conferred briefly, then the younger of them turned to the taxi and studied the line of bullet holes in its side. They began just in front of the rear seats, and Lorimer didn't need anybody to tell him he was lucky he hadn't been killed. Perhaps when he dived to the floor the gunman had assumed he was hit.

The older policeman was talking to the men from the Cadillac. Probably asking them if they had seen what happened, Lorimer guessed. They might have noticed the Mercedes, but he doubted if they had seen anything else; the gunman's pistol hadn't projected more than two or three inches outside the window, and the German car had been some distance away. It was unlikely they had heard anything, either, above the noise of the traffic.

Apparently they hadn't, and their main concern seemed to be the damage done to the Cadillac when the taxi hit it. The policeman's manner was deferential. He said something to his colleague and walked over to their car. Lorimer saw him using its radio and wished he could hear what he was saying. But if he had, he wouldn't have understood it, he thought. He remembered Grantley's telling him that one reason why he had been chosen to come out here was the time he had spent in the Sudan ten years ago, the implication being that he would at least be able to make himself understood. It was bloody ironic. The first sign of trouble, when he really needed to make himself clear, and he was as helpless as a boxer with no arms.

The remnants of the crowd, which had been quiet for the last two or three minutes, began muttering again. The taxi driver, propped up in the passenger seat now, had stopped groaning and looked surly. When the younger policeman began questioning him he answered in monosyllables. It seemed to Lorimer he wasn't receiving much sympathy. Maybe the police already knew him.

The older of them returned. "You go to gaol," he said in a flat voice to Lorimer.

"Gaol?" Lorimer was outraged. "What the hell for? I've been shot at and nearly killed, and I saved that man's life."

The younger policeman laughed as if it were a great joke. "Not gaol," he explained. "Station. You go to police station with me."

"Oh," Lorimer said. He knew he had no alternative, but also that he probably had nothing to lose by going except an hour or so of his time. There might be somebody at the police station who spoke more English, or who, at least, would call in an interpreter. He retrieved his bag from the back of the Peugeot, and, taking two notes from his wallet, gave them to the driver, who accepted them with no more than a baleful look.

"Come," the policeman said.

He began pushing a way between the few spectators who remained. Their number had dwindled further as it became clear nothing exciting was going to happen and the driver wasn't seriously injured. A few yards away, the driver of the Cadillac and his companion were deep in conversation with the other policeman.

Despite the wail of its siren, the journey into the city in the police car was smoother and more comfortable than in the taxi. It took

fifteen minutes, and in that time Lorimer's escort spoke only once, on
his radio.

Beyond the outer suburbs the modern skyscrapers gave way to
traditional ochre-coloured buildings. Then the car turned left into a
maze of old streets, turning several more times before finally stopping
outside a narrow building with barred windows. It looked like a
prison, Lorimer thought. A flagpole jutted out over the street above
the entrance, and from it the Shajihan flag hung limply, as if it, too,
found the heat oppressive.

"You out," the policeman said, more politely than the words implied.

He ushered Lorimer into a bare room with a single barred window
set high in one wall, a table, and benches along two of the other walls,
said curtly, "Wait," and left him.

Lorimer waited a long time. The ancient fan suspended from the
ceiling wasn't working, and the heat, combined with a stench he
preferred not to try to analyse, sapped his energy. All he wanted was
to be out of that fetid room, relaxing in a bath at the Excelsior. He
could hear the scrape of shoes on a stone floor as people moved about
in the corridor, and once or twice a snatch of talk or a voice raised in
protest. Outside in the street small boys shrieked joyfully, and once a
man in the police uniform looked into the room, then disappeared
again without speaking. No one else came.

Time became an obsession. What the hell were they doing? They
couldn't suspect him of shooting the taxi driver, the bullet holes had
been clear enough in the side of the Peugeot. One of the policemen
had examined them, he must have seen they had been fired from
outside the cab. Anyway, the driver would surely have told them what
happened. So why didn't they take his statement, or whatever it was
they wanted, and let him go?

The room was reasonably clean, yet he felt dirty. His shirt was
sticking to his back, his trousers in his crotch. There was a band of
perspiration round his waist. The window was too high for him to see
through it, and after a while he sat down on the bench. As far as he
could see, there was nothing to prevent his walking out. Somehow he
could find his way to a main street, hail a taxi and tell the driver to
take him to the Excelsior. But it would be stupid to do that. Apart
from anything else, the police had his passport.

It was over an hour before anybody came for him. Then it was the young policeman who had brought him there. "You come with me?" he said.

Resisting a temptation to ask why he had been kept waiting so long, Lorimer followed him along a corridor and up some stairs to another room. It was very different from the one he had just left. A large fan in the middle of the ceiling revolved lazily with a gentle sighing sound, and the air, free of odours, was pleasantly cool. There were rugs on the floor, and in the wall facing Lorimer as he entered the room, a large window looked out onto a courtyard behind the building. The furniture was modern, from the large rosewood desk to the leather-and-steel chairs, the wardrobe near the window, and the filing cabinets against another wall. The wall behind the desk was mostly occupied by a map of Shajiha.

The man seated at the desk was wearing a grey Western-style suit. He was a very large man with thin dark hair and strangely smooth cheeks, but it was not only his size that made him impressive, Lorimer thought; his eyes under his thick black brows were shrewd and his small mouth thin-lipped. A formidable man. Possibly a cruel one.

When the two men entered the room, he stood up. The policeman stationed himself just inside the door. In case he tried to make a run for it, Lorimer supposed. But why should he want to now when he had been left unguarded for over an hour downstairs?

"Mr. Lorimer," the big man said. He smiled, revealing very white teeth. "I am Inspector Mahfuz. Sit down, please. I am sorry you were kept waiting so long, but there were certain formalities which it was necessary to attend to. How long have you been in our country?"

"About two hours," Lorimer replied coolly.

"It is a pity you have had so unfortunate a reception." Mahfuz spoke fluent English with a pronounced accent. "Why have you come to Dhartoum?"

Lorimer repeated what he had told the immigration officer at the airport.

"You work for this company Maxwells?"

"For the company which owns them."

"Ah yes, United."

The Inspector nodded and glanced down at a paper on his desk. Lorimer guessed it was the policeman's report, and that Mahfuz was sounding him out. It explained why they had kept him kicking his heels so long downstairs when they couldn't seriously suspect him of the shooting. They must have been in touch with the airport, and possibly with one of their ministries and Maxwells' local office, too.

"It was very sad, Mr. O'Brien taking his own life like that. You knew him?"

"No," Lorimer said.

Mahfuz eyed him thoughtfully. "Where will you be staying while you are here, Mr. Lorimer?"

"The Excelsior."

"Ah yes. It is an excellent hotel. I am sure you will be very comfortable there."

The big man hardly moved, but Lorimer knew the preliminaries were over, and that now they had come to the real purpose of the interview. Mahfuz's manner was relaxed, almost urbane, but despite it and his apparent friendliness, Lorimer sensed a latent hostility. It wasn't overt racial prejudice, it was more subtle than that, but it was there. Did the Inspector dislike the British, or only this particular Briton?

"Please tell me exactly what happened, Mr. Lorimer."

Lorimer obeyed. It was strange, he thought, how some things, mostly impressions, remained clear in his memory, while others were already hazy. As if his brain was acting as a censor, selecting only parts of what had happened for his memory to retain.

"You are sure it was a Mercedes?" Mahfuz asked when he had finished.

"Yes."

"And green?"

"Light green. And fairly new."

"You didn't see the number?"

"No." Lorimer felt like asking Mahfuz if he had ever been shot at from a speeding car and, if he had, how much he noticed of it.

"That is not surprising." The big man smiled, but again the smile seemed designed to cover a basic antipathy. "The man who fired the shots, you say he was young and dark. You mean he was an Arab?"

"He looked like it to me."

"How old was he?"

"Twenty, twenty-one."

The Inspector pushed the papers on his desk to one side and sat back a little in his chair. "And that is all you can tell me about him?" he asked.

"No."

Overhead the fan sighed softly. Mahfuz waited, saying nothing. But the atmosphere in the room was suddenly more tense.

"He was at the airport," Lorimer said.

"You are sure?"

"Yes. He came up and asked me what my name was. He said he had to meet a Mr. Smith."

He had been thinking about that brief encounter while he was waiting in the hot, stinking room downstairs. It didn't make sense. Nevertheless he was sure he was right. There was no mistaking that disfiguring little scar just below the gunman's left eye.

Mahfuz frowned. "You know nothing of this Mr. Smith?"

"No, except that it's the commonest name in Britain. I don't know any Smith out here. Or anybody else."

"It is clear the young man didn't know him, only that he had been sent to meet him. Smith is an English name. You are English, therefore he asked you if you were Mr. Smith." The Inspector paused. "You are sure it was the same man in the Mercedes? The one who fired the shots?"

"Certain."

"There was a Cadillac following your taxi. The men who were in it are prominent businessmen in Dhartoum. They saw a Mercedes pass them, then the taxi. They say it was going fast until it was level with your cab, then it slowed. They did not hear any shots, but just after it passed the taxi, the taxi swerved badly and hit their car."

"The driver collapsed," Lorimer said. "Why should anyone want to shoot up the taxi?"

"To force it off the road," Mahfuz replied. "Perhaps to injure the driver so that he would not be able to work for a long time. There is always war between our taxi drivers over passengers from the airport. It is very profitable business, and much desired. You have the same trouble at Heathrow, no?"

Not exactly, Lorimer thought. He hadn't heard of taxis being shot at and forced off the M4. But he said nothing.

"Sometimes it is tyres that are cut," Mahfuz went on. "But this is not the first time a driver has been shot or a cab destroyed. Last month two taxis were set on fire here in Dhartoum. Perhaps this that happened today was in revenge for that, I do not know. I am only sorry you had to be involved, a visitor to our country. It is the first time you come here?"

"Yes," Lorimer agreed.

"Then it is even more unfortunate. I assure you, Mr. Lorimer, we do not usually treat our guests so badly. Let us hope the rest of your stay will be as pleasant as the unfortunate circumstances permit." The Inspector stood up. "I am most grateful for your help. Now all that is over, and Assad will drive you to your hotel."

"May I have my passport back?" Lorimer asked.

"Of course. I am sorry." The big man handed it to him and watched him tuck it away in his inside pocket. "Goodbye, Mr. Lorimer. And good luck."

You too, Lorimer thought. Perhaps all those people back in London who had given him their best wishes had known something. Did Mahfuz, too? If so, his troubles weren't over yet. "Goodbye," he said.

Assad held the door open for him, and together they went down the stairs and out to the car, still parked outside the building. This time Assad didn't switch on the siren. They drove through narrow old streets, past women wearing the black *taub* and old men with faces as dark and wrinkled as walnuts. There were no pavements, and children played in the road.

Then, quite suddenly, they were out of the slums of the old town and crossing the wide September Square, named to commemorate the Army coup which, fifteen years before, had ousted the monarchy and installed a socialist government. The Square was dominated by the massive white bulk of the former royal palace, now the official residence of the President. The French architect had apparently been inspired by the Paris Opera House. Facing it was the city's biggest mosque, its great dome surrounded by four minarets.

The Excelsior was just round a corner in Gamal Nasser Street. It was large, modern, and, if you overlooked the enormous mural in the cocktail bar, could as well have been in Sydney or San Francisco. Even the mural, which had been painted by a Danish artist, would have looked more at home in the Egyptian Room of a hotel in the United States. That was no accident, it was what the American group which owned the Excelsior believed the Western businessmen who provided most of its revenue wanted. In such a place they could feel at home and, therefore, secure.

Lorimer registered and took a lift to the eleventh floor. Three more, he told himself, and he would be on a par with Grantley. His room was air-conditioned, comfortable, and as lacking in character as he had expected. From the window there was an extensive view of roof-tops and several mosques. The feeling that he was not only hot, but also dirty, persisted. First things first, he thought. Dropping his bag on the stand, he went into the bathroom and turned on both bath-taps. Afterwards he would ring Mrs. O'Brien and let her know he was here.

Lying in the bath he thought about all that had happened. Too many people were taking an interest in him. First there had been Grantley, picking him for this job for no very satisfactory reason. Then the Arab gunman. Now Mahfuz. The Inspector's story about a taxi war might be true, but Lorimer was convinced that the shots this afternoon weren't part of it; the young Arab with the scar had picked him out at the airport. He hadn't asked if he was Mr. Smith, he had said, "What is your name, please?" At the time Lorimer had put it down to the young man's limited English, but now it seemed revealing. And there was another thing. The Arab hadn't waited for the man he was supposed to meet; as soon as he knew Lorimer's name, he had hurried out of the terminal building.

Somebody wanted him dead. But why should anybody here want to kill him? It didn't make sense.

FOUR

The Carlton was an older and smaller hotel than the Excelsior and, as it was only a quarter of a mile away, Lorimer walked there after dinner.

Janet O'Brien had told him on the telephone that she would meet him in the lobby. He spotted her at once, a big-boned, fleshy woman, a little above average height, with dark brown hair and dark eyes. She was no longer the pretty girl she had been once, but she looked trim and quite attractive standing near the porters' cubby-hole in a pale-green-and-white dress and white sandals. Apparently she felt no need to wear any sort of mourning.

She noticed him at the same moment, and he saw her hesitate, uncertain whether she should come to meet him. In the end she compromised, taking a token couple of steps towards him.

"Mrs. O'Brien?" he said.

"Yes. You're Mr. Lorimer." Her voice was plummy and slightly affected, the voice of a woman who had moved up in the world and felt it necessary to change her natural way of speaking.

Lorimer hadn't been looking forward to their meeting. Her grief was a barrier between them, invisible, but none the less real for that, and her manner now suggested that she was torn between a desire to make plain her status as the widow of a divisional manager and a need to confide in him.

"I'm very sorry," he told her.

"Yes. Thank you." There were signs of strain in Janet's face, but she seemed to have her emotions under control.

"Is there anywhere we can talk?"

She looked round uncertainly. "They don't like women in the bar, and there isn't a lounge. We could go to the Square, there are some seats there."

"Shall we do that then?" Lorimer suggested.

They went out by the revolving door into the hot, airless street. The pavement was crowded, so that they had to walk in single file, and once or twice Janet glanced back over her shoulder as if to make sure Lorimer was still following her.

At the corner of the Square she stopped. Cars raced past, horns blaring, and the hordes of cyclists seemed to bear a charmed life. Then the traffic lights changed, everything came to a sudden halt, and Janet and Lorimer crossed the road.

In the middle of the Square tall trees surrounded an open space in the centre of which stood an impressive memorial to the leader of the revolution. There were some seats, and the trees provided a little shade.

"Shall we sit here?" Janet asked.

She appeared unsure of herself, Lorimer thought. As if her self-confidence had been undermined. If so, it wasn't surprising; her husband's suicide must have come as a terrible blow to her. Perhaps she blamed herself for having failed him in some way she might not understand herself.

They sat down and he kicked away an empty Coca-Cola can, sending a small cloud of dust shin-high. Even here, it seemed, progress had brought with it some of the incidentals of Western life.

"I suppose they told you what he did," Janet said.

"Yes." She was forcing herself to face up to it because she knew that sooner or later she would have to, and it was better to talk about it than have it remain an unspoken horror haunting her. Very likely this was the first opportunity she had had to talk to anybody except the police and Maxwells' manager. Perhaps his being a stranger helped, Lorimer thought. "Did he leave a letter?" he asked gently.

Janet didn't answer immediately. She was watching the dust her own shoes had disturbed, and it seemed her thoughts were far away. "No," she said at last, "he didn't leave anything."

Perhaps that made it harder for her to bear what he had done. She might feel that at the end he had rejected her. Perhaps had known she couldn't help him. Or wouldn't? A letter, some sort of explanation, might have helped her now, but you couldn't blame a man driven to the limits of his endurance and beyond for not considering that. Only try to understand, and do what you could to minimize the damage he had caused.

"I'm sorry," Lorimer said, "but I have to ask. Have you any idea why he did it?"

"He was worried, depressed," Janet answered, so quietly Lorimer hardly heard her above the noise of the traffic.

"About his work?"

"Yes, of course. What else could it have been?" She sounded alarmed. "Oh, you think it might have been us. That we—"

"No, I didn't mean that. He could have been worried about money, or his health," Lorimer said.

"I don't know," Janet muttered. "He trusted people. Sometimes they let him down."

"Somebody had let him down out here? A customer?"

"No. Oh, I don't know. It all got too much for him."

It was vague, possibly no more than a distraught widow's imaginings, but if a deal had gone wrong, it might mean Maxwells were at risk. And for O'Brien to have killed himself, he must have been implicated in more than an error of judgement. Had Grantley suspected something of the sort?

"He didn't say anything?" Lorimer asked.

"He never talked about his work. I don't know anything about it." There was a note of desperation in Janet's voice. More calmly she added, "I think his brother's being killed affected him, too. They were very close."

"His brother?" Lorimer asked.

"He was shot in Northern Ireland. Pat was four years younger than Mike, he was only thirty-two when he died."

O'Brien was forty-two. Which meant his brother had been killed six years ago. No doubt he had been affected, but surely not enough after all this time for it to play any part in his committing suicide? Lorimer remembered the photograph in O'Brien's file; that wasn't the face of a man who brooded uselessly. Janet had hinted he might have done, and she had been very quick to say she knew nothing about his work. Did she suspect something was wrong there? Oh well, that was one of the things he was here to look into.

"There'll be arrangements to make," he said quietly. "I'll see to everything I can. Where do you want the funeral to be?"

"Oh, at home. Mike would have wanted that. But it'll be a cremation." Janet paused, and when she went on it seemed almost as if she
had rehearsed the words in advance, like an actor learning his lines.
"It's been a terrible shock. Everything seemed to be going so well.
But if he was going to do it, I'm not surprised he did it there. He
liked that headland; he took me up there the first evening we were
here."

Lorimer waited a moment before he said, "If there's anything I can
do, that's partly what I'm here for."

"Yes, thank you. Mr. Oldfield said I wasn't to worry about money. I
don't suppose there'll be much, except one or two insurance policies.
Neither of us had any money of our own." Janet looked away between
the trees to the traffic endlessly circling the Square. "I talked to our
children yesterday, but I couldn't . . ." She stopped. "I'd like to go
back to the hotel now, if you don't mind."

"Yes, of course," Lorimer agreed. He would learn no more now.

They walked slowly, hardly speaking. When they reached the Carlton, Janet held out her hand and said, "Goodbye, Mr. Lorimer."

"I'll let you know as soon as I've been able to arrange anything," he
promised.

"Yes, thank you." As if it had been building up inside her and she
could no longer hold it back, Janet burst out, "I hate this country. I
hate the people, everything about it."

She turned and walked quickly into the hotel.

Lorimer returned to the Excelsior. He was tired. It was the heat, he
told himself, and perhaps the reaction after all that had happened.
One drink in the bar, then he would be ready for bed. Tomorrow he
must go in to Maxwells' office. He wondered idly what Melissa Forster was doing this evening. He wouldn't have minded being with her.

The Excelsior's big lobby was hardly busy. Two German businessmen were registering at the reception desk, and a middle-aged American was talking to one of the porters, but apart from three or four of
the staff, they were the only people in sight. Lorimer turned left into
the bar, which, by comparison, was crowded. As he stood looking
round for a vacant table, a man in a khaki uniform who had been
standing near one of the pillars watching the door strolled over.

"Mr. Lorimer?" he asked.

Lorimer took in his uniform, and his spirits sank. "Yes?" he said.

"I am Inspector Hassan. I would like a few minutes' talk with you, please." The Inspector's English was almost faultless, with practically no accent.

"What about?" Lorimer demanded. The last thing he felt like just now was another session of police questioning. He studied the other man. Hassan was about forty, he guessed. Of medium height, but slim, with lean features, a rather aquiline nose, and thoughtful eyes. His jaw, though, was strong, and there was nothing weak about his rather thin-lipped mouth. It was a strangely contradictory face, Lorimer thought, that of an idealist with a streak of ruthlessness. It could be a dangerous combination. "I told Inspector Mahfuz everything I know this afternoon," he said.

"I know what you told Inspector Mahfuz," Hassan agreed politely. "I would still like to talk to you."

"Very well." Sighing, Lorimer bowed to the inevitable. "There's a table over there."

"Not here. It would be better if we went up to your room."

"Why?"

Hassan smiled faintly. "It will be more private. I assure you, that's the only reason. If you would like to have a drink first, I will wait."

Suddenly a drink seemed less attractive to Lorimer. Afterwards, probably, he would want one again, maybe more than one, but for the present his only wish was to get rid of this new policeman as quickly as he could.

"It will keep," he said.

Hassan waited for him to go out to the lobby first. A lift was coming down, and while they waited for it Lorimer saw one of the clerks behind the reception desk eyeing them curiously. He wondered whether tomorrow, if he wasn't in gaol by then, he would be asked to find another hotel. But perhaps the Excelsior's staff were used to the police questioning their guests.

The lift stopped and two Arab women got out. They wore Western clothes, and their faces were beautifully made up. Seeing Hassan, one of them murmured something to her companion, who laughed. Lorimer was amused to see that Hassan looked slightly embarrassed, and wondered what exactly the woman had said; the gist of it was clear enough. He noticed that the Inspector hadn't needed to ask which floor, pressing the button for the eleventh as soon as they got into the lift.

They travelled upwards in silence. When they reached his room, Lorimer stood back for Hassan to enter it first.

"Well?" he demanded. "What is it you want to talk about?"

"A few questions, that's all." Hassan must have sensed his hostility, but he didn't seem to mind it, and he himself was very relaxed.

Lorimer took the easy chair and left the less comfortable one for Hassan. The Inspector had forced his company on him, he owed him nothing. Rather, it was the other way round.

"It's about what happened this afternoon, I suppose," he said.

"No. That is Inspector Mahfuz's case, I have nothing to do with it."

"His case? The taxi war, you mean?"

"He told you about that?"

"Yes."

Their eyes met. "Mr. O'Brien was a friend of yours?" Hassan asked.

"I'd never met him."

"Then why are you here?"

"I explained all that to Inspector Mahfuz. I'm the personal assistant to the managing director of another company in the Group. They wanted somebody to tidy up anything he hadn't finished and look after Mrs. O'Brien. I was available."

"Surely Maxwells' staff here could have handled that?"

"I expect so."

"So why send you?"

"I wish I knew," Lorimer said. He asked himself why Hassan irritated him. Was it his questions, duplicating Mahfuz's, or his manner, cool, correct and absolutely impersonal? And disbelieving. Perhaps it was neither of them, but his own weariness.

"You still say you didn't know Mr. O'Brien?"

"I told you, I never met him. Did you?"

The Inspector ignored the question. "You met his wife this evening."

"You had me followed," Lorimer said angrily.

Hassan stood up and walked to the window. Then, turning, he asked, "Did she tell you why her husband killed himself?"

"She said he was depressed. He'd been under a lot of strain because of his work."

The Inspector's expression didn't change, but Lorimer sensed a quickening of his interest. He knew in that moment that this was really why Hassan had come. Not to question him about himself, but to find out all he knew about O'Brien. It was as simple as that. O'Brien had committed suicide, and they wanted to know the whys and wherefores in order to complete their records. They had no interest in the dead man himself, to them he was merely a body to be shipped home to Britain as soon as possible; they were concerned solely with their own bureaucratic procedures. Lorimer was mildly disgusted.

Then he saw there might be another motive: The Shajihan authorities didn't want people in Britain alleging that O'Brien had been murdered and they had bungled the inquiries.

"That's probably true," Hassan agreed, his tone so devoid of expression it had to be deliberate.

Lorimer eyed him keenly. "Why should she lie?" he demanded.

"I have said, I do not think she was lying." Abruptly Hassan changed the direction of his questioning. "The man you say shot at you this afternoon, would you recognize him again?"

"Yes."

"You are so sure? You can't have seen him for more than a few seconds at the most, and he was holding a gun."

"He had a scar just below his left eye. It was pretty distinctive."

"Ah yes, of course." Hassan looked thoughtful.

You disbelieving sod, Lorimer thought. "You don't believe he exists, do you?" he asked. "You think I made it all up, and I shot the driver myself."

Hassan smiled. "No, Mr. Lorimer, I believe you. I've seen the driver's statement and the policemen's report. They are quite clear about the bullet holes in the taxi, and that they were fired from outside it. I am curious, that's all."

"I thought it wasn't your case."

"Nor is it. Unless . . ." Hassan paused. "I wonder why you."

"Not half as much as I do," Lorimer told him with feeling.

"No, I don't suppose so." Again the Inspector permitted himself a faint smile. "It must have been an alarming experience."

"The man who fired those shots asked me my name at the airport. As if he were picking me out. And he didn't wait for the Mr. Smith he said he was meeting; as soon as he knew who I was, he walked straight out of the building."

"That is partly what makes me wonder."

"Wonder what?"

But again Hassan changed the subject. Did he ever answer a question? Lorimer wondered. "Your Mr. O'Brien, how much do you know about his work in Shajiha?"

"Not much. Maxwells are a transport company, and they own some ships. Also they supply oil and gas installations."

Hassan nodded. "That I knew."

"O'Brien was their Overseas Manager. He was responsible for seeing all their local offices outside Britain did their job properly, so he travelled a lot."

"Do you know how long he had been here on this trip?"

"About a week. Why? What about it? He came out fairly regularly."

"Often," Hassan observed, "rather than regularly, I think. It was only three months since his last visit, and seven months since the one before that."

"So?" It was oftener than Lorimer would have expected, but presumably O'Brien knew what he was doing. His recent reports all said he was a good manager, there must have been a reason for his visiting a comparatively minor branch of Maxwells' network so often. A doubt about the local management, perhaps. Or local contacts to be renewed and "commissions" to be agreed. Personal relationships were especially important in the Middle East. It could have been a dozen things. One it certainly wasn't: He couldn't have come for the climate.

"Three nights ago," Hassan said evenly, "he was seen acting suspiciously in the immediate vicinity of a highly secret base."

FIVE

Lorimer stared at him. Clearly Hassan wasn't joking. The Middle East was a vulnerable area, to put it mildly, and it was understandable if people were a bit edgy where security was concerned. To them a foreigner's being within several miles of a military installation might well have a sinister connotation.

"What do you mean, acting suspiciously?" he asked. "Was he taking photographs, or just having a casual look?"

"It was no casual look," Hassan replied. "The camp is nearly two hundred kilometres from here, and one hundred from the nearest village of any size. There is no apparent reason for his going anywhere near it. Nevertheless he parked his car a kilometre away, hidden in some sandhills, and walked towards it. It is believed he was taking photographs."

Lorimer was shaken. If this was true, and it didn't sound like the imaginings of a jittery command, it was serious. Bloody serious. God knew what the consequences might be. Was it possible O'Brien had been working for British Intelligence?

Not long ago the idea would have seemed so unlikely as to be ridiculous, but a lot of veils had been torn aside lately. After all, he had the classic cover. Could that be why Grantley was taking a personal interest in his suicide? Because he knew?

Lorimer remembered what Janet had told him, that people had let down her husband. No wonder he was under a lot of pressure if he was out here on a mission and knew he had been left without support, even betrayed.

"I don't believe it," he said.

"That he was near the camp, or that he was a spy?" Hassan showed no resentment; Lorimer's response had been predictable.

"That he was up to anything. He probably saw the place as he drove past and went back to see what it was." If so, he was a damned fool.

"That's possible," Hassan agreed. "But I don't think it's likely. He seems to have approached it from the north, and from that direction you can't see it until you are past the dunes where he left his car."

Lorimer understood: O'Brien had known the camp was there. His motive might still have been nothing more sinister than curiosity, but he didn't believe it. To drive four hundred kilometres late in the evening didn't sound like mere inquisitiveness.

"When a searchlight was switched on, he turned and ran back to his car," Hassan continued.

"I don't blame him. Wouldn't you?"

"What I would do doesn't matter, Mr. Lorimer. I am concerned only with Mr. O'Brien. And you."

"Just a minute," Lorimer objected. "If it was dark enough for them to use a searchlight, he can't have been taking photographs."

"There are techniques, special film and so on," Hassan said. "But that isn't important. What matters is why he went out there."

"I don't accept he was doing anything wrong," Lorimer told him, his coolness matching Hassan's. "But if he was, he would hardly tell anyone. Not Maxwells. He'd keep it between him and whoever he was working for."

"Perhaps." Hassan came back into the middle of the room, but he didn't sit down.

"So why are you interested in me?"

"For several reasons. That is one of them. Another is why the young man with a scar shot at you this afternoon. One shot might perhaps be intended as a warning, even high spirits, but a burst with an automatic weapon aimed at a taxi is something else. We don't have trigger-happy militias in Dhartoum; it seems he meant to kill you."

"I'd worked that out," Lorimer agreed warmly. "But why me? I've never been to Shajiha before, and I don't know anybody here. I'd never met O'Brien—I hadn't even heard of him before yesterday—and until then I didn't know myself I was coming."

Hassan shrugged. "I don't know why, Mr. Lorimer. But if I were you, I would keep a low profile while you are here. And I would finish my business and go back to England as soon as I could."

"Is that an official warning?"

"Not official, no. But it's quite serious. I would advise you to pay regard to it." The Inspector paused. "I would like you to come to my office to look at some photographs and see if you can identify the man who shot at you."

For a policeman who had nothing to do with that business he was taking a lot of interest in it, Lorimer thought. But he had said it wasn't his case "unless . . ." Then he had stopped. Unless what? Had it something to do with O'Brien's supposed activities?

"All right," he agreed. "When?"

"Tomorrow afternoon?" Hassan suggested. "I will send a car here for you at three o'clock. Good night, Mr. Lorimer." He walked to the door.

"This camp," Lorimer said. "Is it an army base?"

Hassan regarded him steadily for several seconds. Lorimer, who hadn't expected him to answer, wondered if he was reflecting that the question might be bluff, pretending ignorance when he knew very well what the camp was.

"It's a prison," Hassan said briefly. He went out, closing the door behind him.

Lorimer frowned. Who was Hassan? Something about him suggested he wasn't an ordinary policeman. His questions, too, and that almost casual acknowledgement that he might have an interest in the shooting this afternoon, sounded more like the local equivalent of the Special Branch. One thing, anyway, was clear—if it came to it, Hassan would be a formidable adversary.

If he was telling the truth, and Lorimer was inclined to think he was, the police had good reason for suspecting O'Brien. What the hell had Maxwells' manager been up to, hanging about round a prison camp more than a hundred miles out in the desert? Lorimer had no doubt the inmates were political prisoners, and governments that maintained such places tended to be sensitive about them.

The odds were they would never know now what O'Brien had been doing. If the Shajihan government publicly accused him of spying, there would be a denial from London, and that would be that. Relations might be soured for a time, but eventually it would all blow over. The trouble was, Hassan suspected him, too, and Lorimer had no illusions that if the police wanted to detain him, they would not bother about little things like evidence. It would be sufficient that O'Brien was suspected and he worked for the same group.

So what, and who, was behind the attempt to shoot him this afternoon?

Lorimer remembered he hadn't yet had the drink he was about to buy himself when the Inspector appeared on the scene.

Maxwells' office was on the seventh floor of a modern block half a mile beyond September Square. The staff consisted of Oldfield, the manager, a small, weedy man in his mid-thirties with thin sandy hair that made an untidy fringe across his forehead, large ears and a permanently apologetic manner; a Shajihan assistant a year or two younger who looked sensible and intelligent; and three local girls.

"I'd have rung you at the hotel last night if I'd known you were coming," Oldfield said in his light, rather high-pitched voice. "I didn't get the telex until this morning."

"It doesn't matter," Lorimer told him. "There wasn't anything you could do."

He wasn't impressed with the manager. Oldfield looked as if he had never taken an important decision in his life without agonizing over it for days before and after. He would always do the right thing because he would be scared stiff of upsetting somebody who might make life harder for him if he didn't.

He didn't look reassured now. He stood, only meeting Lorimer's eye when he had to, and fidgeting a little. Lorimer could smell his sweat. It probably meant nothing, he told himself; Oldfield was just one of the world's worriers. And he seemed unperturbed when Lorimer told him he wanted to see the accounts. Nothing suggested a guilty conscience. Why should it? Lorimer thought. It was O'Brien who had committed suicide.

After eyeing him surreptitiously when he walked in, the rest of the staff appeared to be taking no further interest in him. Very likely none of them but the man, Ali Ammar, spoke much English, but he was taking no chances.

"Let's go into your room," he said.

"Yes. Yes, of course," Oldfield agreed, as if apologizing for not suggesting it first.

His office was little more than eight feet square, furnished with a desk, two chairs, a framed photograph of the Queen and a calendar with a picture of Ben Lomond. They sat down, Lorimer facing the desk.

"You know why they've sent me out here?" he asked. Oldfield nodded. "First I want you to tell me everything you can about O'Brien."

The manager looked worried. Lorimer guessed he did his work fairly conscientiously without ever looking beyond the day-to-day routine. He wondered how he coped with the sudden crises every business suffered.

"I don't think there's anything I can tell you," Oldfield said doubtfully.

"How long have you worked here?"

"Just over two years."

"How many times did he come out during that time?"

"I don't know." Oldfield shifted uneasily in his chair. "About six, I suppose."

"Six?" Lorimer was startled. Even Hassan hadn't suggested it was so often.

"Sometimes it would be three months, sometimes nearly six."

"You must know something about him then."

"He was out of the office a lot of the time, seeing customers and that."

"What sort of man was he?"

Clearly Oldfield wasn't used to thinking much about other people. They passed through his life making no more impression on his mind than an automatic liking or dislike. If he had ever thought of O'Brien as a man, instead of as his boss, he had never put his thoughts together.

"He was all right," he answered uncertainly.

"What do you mean, 'all right'?"

"Well, he was easy to get on with. You know."

Lorimer thought he did. O'Brien had been friendly, easygoing and uncritical. He hadn't rocked Oldfield's boat. By temperament as well as training, the Overseas Manager was a salesman, not an accountant or an efficiency expert.

"What did he talk about?" he inquired.

"Nothing much. Just business and ordinary things."

"Was he a cheerful man? Moody?"

"I'd have said he was cheerful. He always seemed it. Happy-go-lucky. You know that sort of Irishman."

"And he was happily married. . . ." Lorimer let the statement hang in the air so that it became a question, almost implying doubt.

"I suppose so. He mentioned his children sometimes. Especially his daughter."

Between the slats of the venetian blind behind Oldfield, Lorimer could see the unbroken blue of the sky and the sun shining on the minarets of the great mosque. The air-conditioning in the office didn't seem to make much difference, the atmosphere was too hot and sultry. The system couldn't be working properly.

"When did you see him last?" Lorimer asked.

"That afternoon."

"How was he then?"

"All right. He seemed a bit worried, as if he'd got something on his mind. But not enough to do what he did." Oldfield hadn't been able to avoid thinking about it a lot over the last three days. "He said something about being glad he was going home, almost as if he was talking to himself. You could see he was looking forward to going."

Lorimer frowned. "You're sure?"

"Oh yes."

Yet within a few hours O'Brien had driven out to the headland, attached a hose to his car's exhaust, and sat in the driver's seat with the windows closed, waiting for the fumes to kill him. Why? What had happened during those last five or six hours to plunge him into such utter despair? Did he learn he was about to be arrested? Hassan hadn't suggested that. Lorimer wondered if Janet knew what it was and wasn't prepared to say.

"Why did he come out here so often?" he asked. "Did he know there was something wrong?" Lorimer didn't believe it, but he knew the suggestion would increase the pressure on Oldfield, and that was the only way he would learn anything useful from him.

"No. I don't know why he came. There isn't anything wrong. He knew that."

"Then why?"

"I said, I don't know. It wasn't my job to question what he did."

Oldfield would never question anything a senior manager did or said, Lorimer thought. No matter how concerned he was, he would keep quiet in case a question brought a rebuff. What it must be like to go through life as scared as that! But maybe he was doing the manager an injustice; if Oldfield had nothing to hide, why should he care how often O'Brien came here? He might even have welcomed his visits as evidence he wasn't forgotten.

"Did you not wonder at all?" he asked, groping in the dark. "He never said anything?"

"I don't know what you're getting at." Oldfield's bewilderment and anxiety made him seem petulant. "He'd just send a telex saying it was about time he paid us another visit and telling me to book a room for him at the Carlton. He always stayed there, he said he liked it better than the big new hotels. When he got here, he just did the usual things. If one of the company's ships was docked, he'd see if there was anything she needed, like extra hands or anything, but most of the time he was out seeing people."

"Customers?"

"And people he thought might give us business."

There was nothing surprising in O'Brien's keeping an eye on Maxwells' ships, Lorimer reflected. The operation out here was his responsibility, and it depended in part on Shipping Division; if they slipped up, he could have problems. Very likely he had an arrangement with Davies, the Shipping Manager.

"The *Maxwell Pride* was here this time," Oldfield volunteered, anxious to appear helpful. "She's the only one comes here much."

Lorimer nodded. "Do you do any work for Shajihan government departments?" he asked.

"One or two: Foreign Trade and Power. And we've done odd jobs for Posts and Communications."

"Nothing for the army or the prison authorities?"

Oldfield looked startled. "No. Mostly it's just shipping general cargo in and out through Dhartoum and arranging transport from the docks. We don't move much stuff inside the country, we've only got one van. We run small loads out to the oilfields, but local firms do the rest." It was clear that being questioned about his work Oldfield felt on firmer ground than when Lorimer wanted him to express an opinion, and he answered more confidently.

"I'll have to look at everything," Lorimer told him. "I might as well start with the books."

"Yes. Yes, of course." The manager hesitated. "If you'd like to work in here, I can easily move outside. There's a spare desk out there I can use."

"Thanks," Lorimer said. "That would be best." He saw no point in telling Oldfield he had intended to take over this room anyway.

Oldfield sent his assistant in with the accounts ledgers. Lorimer was no accountant, and it would have taken one to be sure there was nothing wrong with them, but he had acquired a working knowledge of bookkeeping and he found nothing. In any case, why should O'Brien commit suicide because of a fiddle in the office here? When he asked Oldfield, the manager told him O'Brien had never done more than glance at the books. Moreover, the auditors had been out three months ago, and they had seemed to be satisfied.

Lorimer's usual lunch comprised sandwiches and a pint in the pub round the corner from United's offices. Occasionally he ate in the staff canteen. He didn't know what people did out here, but Hassan had said he would send a car to the Excelsior for him at three, and he had better be there then. In the meantime he might as well see what the hotel could provide in the way of a snack.

The car arrived dead on time. It bore no markings, and Lorimer noticed the wary look the Excelsior's porter gave it.

They crossed September Square, turned right along a wide tree-lined boulevard in the government area of the city, and finally drew up at the side of a building that was imposing even by the standards of its neighbours. That, and the unmarked car, reinforced Lorimer's belief that Hassan was no ordinary policeman. However, such signs as there were were in Arabic, and would probably have told him nothing even if he could read them.

He was taken straight to the Inspector's office on the second floor, up a wide marble staircase and along an elegant corridor. The room, however, was small, fashioned out of part of another, much larger one, and furnished for efficiency rather than elegance. Its air-conditioning was a lot more effective than Oldfield's; despite the fierce heat outside, the air here was pleasantly cool.

When Lorimer was shown in, Hassan stood up and dismissed the driver. "Sit down, Mr. Lorimer," he said. His manner hadn't changed; it was still correct with the hostility thinly veiled.

Lorimer sat on a chair facing the desk.

"You went to Maxwells' office this morning."

"I told you I was going. And I don't like being followed."

For a moment Hassan eyed Lorimer in silence, then he said flatly, "It's better than being dead."

Lorimer was startled. It hadn't occurred to him that the surveillance might be for his protection. He should have remembered that, having failed to kill him yesterday, the gunman with the scar would very likely try again.

"I'll give you that," he agreed.

"I would like you to look at some photographs," Hassan told him.

From films he had seen, Lorimer expected him to produce thick volumes of police "mug shots" for him to wade through. Instead Hassan went across to the safe in a corner of the room, opened it, and took out a thin sheaf of ten-by-eight prints, which he laid on his desk facing Lorimer.

"See if you recognize any of these men," he said.

Lorimer turned the prints over, studying each one carefully. He thought he had rarely seen a more villainous-looking bunch. Most of them he could reject immediately, he was as sure as he could be he had never seen them. But when he came to the last but one, he stopped. Staring up at him from Hassan's desk, stark in black and white, were the thin, almost girlish features of the young man at the airport, the scar marring the smooth olive skin just below his left eye. He felt a slight sense of shock. He had seen the young man for—how long? Twenty seconds?—when he asked him his name, and only a fleeting second or two in the green Mercedes, yet there could be no mistaking his face. At first glance it was far less evil-looking than those in the other pictures, but looking at it more closely, he thought he could see something dangerous there. Perhaps it was in the eyes. And there was a hint of cruelty in that thin-lipped mouth.

"That's the man," he said. He handed the pictures back to Hassan, the young man's on top.

"He is the man who asked you your name at the airport, and later fired at your taxi?"

"Yes."

"You are certain?"

"Positive. Who is he?"

"His name is Saad Hatem."

"You know him?"

"By record, not personally." Hassan returned the photographs to his safe, locked it, and slipped the key into his pocket. "You ask a lot of questions, Mr. Lorimer," he remarked.

Lorimer felt a small tenseness inside him. It was too slight to be alarm, more like anticipation, an awareness that some cards, at least, were being laid on the table. And that he might be treading on dangerous ground. "Too many?" he asked.

"Perhaps. Some questions are better not asked—especially by foreigners."

"I'm interested in who tried to kill me."

Hassan smiled faintly. "That's understandable. Did you learn anything about Mr. O'Brien this morning?"

"Not much."

"He seems to have been a man of mystery."

"I wouldn't say that," Lorimer said easily. "You can't expect the people here to know much about him. He was their boss, they wouldn't see him outside the office, and he only came for a few days at a time."

"Perhaps you are right."

Hassan appeared to brush the subject aside as of little interest. Lorimer was becoming used to his apparently dismissing topics he himself had brought up. He suspected Hassan by no means lost interest in them, he merely put them aside temporarily while he considered something else. Perhaps he didn't want them to seem too important. Or perhaps it was to keep the other person off his guard. Hassan was a very shrewd operator indeed.

For a moment he looked thoughtful as he eyed Lorimer. Then, as if he had reached a decision, he said briskly, "Come with me, Mr. Lorimer. There is something I would like you to see."

Lorimer stood up. "Where are we going?" he asked.

"To the mortuary," Hassan told him.

SIX

The journey in Hassan's official car didn't take long. For Lorimer, it passed too quickly. He supposed Hassan wanted him to look at O'Brien's body, and that was an experience he would have preferred to forgo. Anyway, what did the Inspector hope to gain from it?

"The mortuary is in the Taufik Zagloul Hospital," Hassan explained.

They drove across the centre of the city, through slums to a street on the edge of the new town. To Lorimer the whole area looked like one huge construction site surrounded by ugly new blocks of high-rise flats. Dust hung like a haze in the sultry air, almost blotting out the sun, while the noise of mechanical diggers and pneumatic drills was nearly deafening. The hospital was on the far side, a white tower twenty-nine storeys high with two lower blocks adjoining it.

The driver pulled up beside one of the blocks and Hassan led the way round to the back. Near the far end was a door labelled in Arabic. He opened it, and Lorimer followed him along a narrow corridor to another door at the end. After the heat outside, the air struck icy-cold, and he shivered. In place of the familiar blend of spices and drains, there was the stringent odour of hospitals everywhere.

"What's all this about?" he demanded.

Hassan pushed open the door without answering, and they entered a large room with strip lights and a good deal of white tiling. Two of the walls were lined with what looked like the drawers of large filing cabinets. A man in a white coat came forward. Hassan said something to him and he walked over to one of the drawers and pulled it open.

"Mr. Lorimer," Hassan said.

Reluctantly Lorimer walked up to the tray and its white-shrouded burden. The attendant drew back the sheet.

There was nothing horrifying or, for him, who hadn't known the dead man, even distressing about O'Brien's body, Lorimer thought. He found it hard to imagine this mould of pallid, inert flesh as a living man.

Hassan was lifting O'Brien's head. "Feel here, just behind and above the right ear," he said.

Unwillingly Lorimer obeyed, his cautious fingers exploring the scalp through the dark, almost black hair. He felt something and frowned. "There's a wound," he said. "A depression."

Hassan drew the sheet back over the dead man's face and nodded to the attendant.

"That's what you brought me here to find?"

"Yes."

Hassan said no more, and Lorimer waited until they were outside in the heat of the hospital car-park before he said, "You think he was murdered. That he was knocked out and put in the car before the pipe was fixed to the exhaust and the engine started."

Hassan nodded. "I believe so."

They began walking slowly back towards his car.

"Couldn't it have happened when his head fell back as he lost consciousness?" Lorimer asked.

"There was nothing there to cause that sort of injury, only the head restraint and the padded seat. Whatever hit him was rounded, fairly thick, and probably heavy."

"Hasn't there been a post-mortem?"

"Oh yes."

"Surely the doctor found that?"

"He did."

Lorimer stopped. "What are you trying to tell me?" he demanded.

Hassan hesitated. "Mr. O'Brien was found dead in his car with a pipe leading from the exhaust, the windows closed, and the engine running. The cause of death was carbon-monoxide poisoning. His wife said he had been depressed, under a lot of pressure lately, and he knew he had been seen in suspicious circumstances near the camp at Al Faktum."

"How did he know?"

"The sentry fired warning shots. He must have believed he was likely to be arrested and charged with spying. It was a clear case of suicide, tragic but sadly all too common."

"What about the pathologist's report?" Lorimer persisted.

"Our police are overworked. Mr. O'Brien was a foreigner, here only for a few days. And almost certainly involved in criminal activities. Perhaps, even, he got the wound before. In any case, it wasn't what killed him. You must see the temptation to ignore it."

"And that's all?" Lorimer demanded.

Hassan shrugged. "Perhaps." They had reached the car and he opened the door for Lorimer to get in. "We will go back to my office."

The journey seemed even shorter this time, and it passed in silence.

"You have a fine building," Lorimer remarked as they got out of the car.

Hassan nodded. "It was once the city house of the King's younger brother," he said.

Nobody seemed to be about as they went up to his office, and their steps rang on the marble stairs. Perhaps the overworked police were all out on duty, or too busy to leave their offices, Lorimer thought. But the people who worked here weren't ordinary CID men and traffic police, were they?

Once in his own room with the door closed, Hassan's manner changed. He seemed to relax, yet at the same time there was a new intensity about him. He didn't speak, just sat in his chair at the desk regarding Lorimer as if still uncertain how much he should tell him.

"You said O'Brien was seen near a prison camp the night before he died," Lorimer said. "You think he was some sort of spy, don't you?"

"It is possible. Just as it is possible you have been sent here to carry on whatever he was doing."

"I don't believe he was doing anything."

"In this case, what you believe may not be relevant, even if you are right. Guns and bullets don't take account of such niceties." The Inspector's tone was brutally matter-of-fact.

"I suppose it's no use my saying I haven't been sent for anything except what I've told you?" Lorimer said.

"No," Hassan agreed. "However, that doesn't matter just now."

Lorimer was angry. But he knew, as he had known while he was waiting in that hot, fetid room at the police station yesterday, that to give vent to his anger would achieve nothing, and might not help much, to put it mildly. "If you really thought he was a spy, you'd have arrested him," he said. "You'd have staged a show trial to warn other people not to try the same thing. You'd have welcomed the chance to demonstrate Shajihan justice."

"I won't argue with you about justice." Hassan's tone was suddenly harsh. "Like beauty, it is often in the eyes of the beholder. And sometimes justice and politics are intertwined, even in England. Our countries are on good terms, a trial of a British subject for espionage might not be opportune."

"Then why not deport him quietly, and make sure he never came back? With a strongly worded note to the British government?"

Hassan shrugged. "I'm not a politician, or a diplomat. I don't know why, only what some people may have thought."

Lorimer stared at him. "Who is Saad Hatem?" he asked.

"A professional gunman. What the Americans call a hit man."

"Are you going to arrest him?"

"On what charge? There is only your word he spoke to you at the airport and fired at your taxi. He would say, why should he? You had only just arrived, you are a stranger here. He had never seen you, never even heard of you; you must have mistaken somebody else for him."

"Do you think I did?" Lorimer demanded.

Hassan smiled a little grimly. "What I think isn't always relevant either. The taxi driver says he saw no Mercedes, nor the man who fired at you. By this time Hatem will have disposed of the gun, and his friends will swear he was with them all yesterday afternoon."

"Who are his friends?"

"Powerful men with influence."

"Maybe they'll pay for my funeral if he succeeds next time," Lorimer said.

"I wouldn't joke about such things," Hassan rebuked him. "About possibilities, yes, but with probabilities it may be tempting Fate, as you say."

Thank you very much, Lorimer thought. Hassan wasn't the person he would most like to visit him if he were seriously ill, he wasn't exactly a ray of sunshine. "Do you want me any more?" he inquired. He wanted to go away, to think quietly about all he had learned. And what he hadn't.

"Not for the present." Hassan stood up and escorted him to the

door. There he said suddenly, "I should like you to have dinner with
my wife and me this evening, Mr. Lorimer. She doesn't often have
the opportunity to talk to people from Britain, she would be very
pleased to meet you. Will you come?"

Lorimer was too startled to answer immediately. The last thing he
had expected from Hassan was any sort of friendly gesture; why
should he invite him if it wasn't to question him when his defences
were down? His first inclination was to decline as politely as he could.
But what had he to lose by accepting? He might even have something
to gain. After all, he was hiding nothing. It would be interesting to
see inside a Shajihan home, and he was beginning to have a sneaking
regard for the Inspector.

"Thank you, I'd like to come," he said.

"Good. I'll call for you at the Excelsior at eight, then. Will that be
all right?"

"Fine."

Still slightly bemused, Lorimer walked down the wide staircase and
across September Square to the Excelsior.

Hassan's own car was a fairly new Rover. He himself was wearing a
short-sleeved shirt, open at the neck, and pale-fawn trousers. It was
the first time Lorimer had seen him out of uniform. Yet, even so
informally dressed, there was still an almost military neatness about
his appearance, as if he could never quite slough off the disciplines of
his job. Perhaps he had no wish to.

They drove through old streets in some of which whole areas of
mud-brick houses were being razed and turned into vast building
sites. They spoke very little; for his part, Lorimer was content to look
out at the passing scene, and Hassan appeared to be preoccupied.

Lorimer could tell by the sun that they were driving westwards.
After a while they came to a new suburb. Here the houses were small,
square boxes without any pretensions to beauty, many of them with
reinforcing rods sticking up from the edges of their flat roofs like
decayed needle teeth, awaiting the time when a second storey might
be added. Beyond them were unlovely grey blocks of workers' flats
like those near the hospital. Dhartoum, Lorimer thought, was losing
its old character fast and becoming a modern city that was almost
incidentally Muslim, just as it might have been incidentally Christian

or Hindu. Perhaps that was what most of its people wanted; ugly or not, the flats must be a vast improvement on the hovels they replaced.

They passed an impressive new stadium.

"Sport is very important here now," Hassan remarked, seeing Lorimer eyeing it. "This year we beat Egypt at soccer."

Lorimer wondered how anybody could play football in the Shajihan climate.

Beyond the stadium the suburbs looked comparatively affluent. The roads were lined with flowering trees, and between them Lorimer could see European-style houses, each with its small garden. After a few minutes Hassan slowed and turned off the road, stopping beside a pleasant house bright with fresh paint and the yellow blossoms of an oleander.

A woman Lorimer judged to be in her late thirties came out to meet them. She was wearing a blouse with long, filmy sleeves and a plain skirt, and with her auburn hair, her short nose and her paler complexion, she looked British or Scandinavian rather than Arabic. There were a sparkle and a serenity about her, so that Lorimer thought here was a happy woman, and also one who felt secure.

"Hallo, Mr. Lorimer," she greeted him. Her voice was low and pleasant, and she spoke English without any trace of an accent. Seeing his expression, she laughed. "Didn't Ahmad tell you?"

"No," Lorimer admitted.

"He wanted to surprise you." She turned to her husband. "You should have done, darling. It wasn't fair."

Hassan smiled complacently.

"He likes surprising visitors from Britain," his wife explained. "Not that we see many."

"You're English," Lorimer said.

"I was, my home was in a village just outside Cambridge. I used to work in a bank there. But I've been Shajihan for a long time now."

She led the way into a room dominated by a three-piece suite covered in a brightly coloured fabric, the wooden legs richly ornamented with gilt.

"We have a girl comes in most days, but she's gone home," she explained. "So I'm seeing to dinner. It won't be long, but I'm afraid you'll have to excuse me or it'll spoil."

Hassan asked Lorimer if he would like a beer.

"Thank you," Lorimer answered. "I thought you wouldn't drink."

"Why not? It isn't against the law. Most Shajihans drink in moderation." Hassan went out of the room, returning almost immediately with two cans and glasses. "It's not quite like real ale, I'm afraid," he commented. "Cheers."

"Cheers," Lorimer said. He had the feeling that events were slipping past him and he was swimming out of his depth. There was something surrealistic about it all—the invitation to dinner, Hassan's wife being British, the apparent change in his attitude towards him. It was absurd he should be sitting here, drinking Hassan's imported Heineken and casually chatting like this.

"Why did you ask me here?" he wanted to know.

"My wife likes meeting people from England," Hassan replied innocently. "She feels it helps her to keep in touch."

"That wasn't the only reason."

"No." Hassan paused, and when he spoke again his bantering tone had gone. "This is a very old country, yet it is almost as if it were new. You British may not have done as much as you might for your colonies, but the countries that occupied us for a hundred years before 1939 did nothing. Less than nothing; they took a lot out and gave next to nothing back. And after the last of them had gone, the old monarchy remained. A monarchy they had installed. We were like a country in your Middle Ages. Before that. Ruled, not governed. Then, in 1969, there was a revolution, and suddenly we were part of the twentieth century. Too suddenly for some people, so that now there are divisions, not only in politics, but in moral attitudes also. Some want us to go the way of Iran, to be a fundamentalist Islamic state; some to be Marxist, and yet others prefer for us to be moderate and socialist, Islamic, but not too narrowly. They take Egypt for their model. It is what the majority of people want, and that is the way we have gone. Women have equal rights and, nominally at least, equal opportunities. They no longer wear the veil unless they wish to, and they can train to be doctors and engineers. Even policewomen. There is free education, and a health service for everyone."

"What's that got to do with your asking me here this evening?" Lorimer inquired.

"A great deal. I'm proud of my country and what it's achieving, but that doesn't mean there aren't things here I don't like. I'm not blind, and in some ways I can look at the situation as an outsider. That can be an advantage, but it makes some things harder to live with." Hassan paused for a moment. "There are things I want to say I couldn't tell you at my office."

"Because the wrong people might overhear them?" Lorimer suggested. In a country like Shajiha, he thought, there would always be people ready to bear tales of disloyalty, real or imagined.

"That's always a possibility." Hassan drank some more of his beer. "O'Brien wasn't murdered for any money he was carrying; his wallet was still in his pocket when he was found and there was a wad of notes in it."

"You think the murder's connected with his being seen near that camp, don't you?" Lorimer asked.

"I think it's likely."

"And that Hatem tried to shoot me because I work for the same group as O'Brien."

"No, because the people who had him killed believe your connection with him was much closer than that."

"That I was sent out here to carry on whatever he was doing?"

"Yes."

"I told you, I know less about him than you do," Lorimer protested.

"So they over-reacted," Hassan agreed equably.

"Thanks very much. When did you stop thinking I was part of the same set-up as O'Brien? Assuming there is one."

"This afternoon. There were too many things you seemed not to understand. The danger you were in, for one. If you were involved, after what happened on the way from the airport, you would have been much more on your guard."

There was something in that, Lorimer reflected. As it was, he still found it hard to believe anybody had really tried to kill him. "Who is Saad Hatem?" he asked. "Apart from being a professional hit man?"

"He's a member of a paramilitary group," Hassan replied. "They call themselves Hizbollah, the Party of God, after the lot in Lebanon. They follow the Iranian line in everything, and they have powerful supporters, here and in other countries. Very powerful. There are plenty of people with a vested interest in de-stabilizing this country, just like any other part of the Middle East. You asked this afternoon if

I was going to arrest Hatem, and I told you the taxi driver swore he saw nothing of him or the Mercedes. If he could have denied the bullet holes in his cab, he would probably have done so."

"You mean he was bribed?"

"No. He wouldn't have taken you if he had known his cab was going to be shot up, he'd have been too scared, and there was no time for anybody to get to him afterwards before the police took his statement. It's just that he knows when it's wise to be ignorant. And today or tomorrow, or maybe the day after, he will receive a generous present, compensation for all he has suffered. It'll be delivered to his house by a stranger who doesn't know who sent it. If I arrested Hatem, he would be free within an hour."

For a second or two there was silence in the over-furnished room. Lorimer could hear Mrs. Hassan moving about in the kitchen. Something bothered him.

"Who are the prisoners?" he asked.

SEVEN

Hassan regarded him blankly, as if his thoughts were a long way off. "Prisoners?" he repeated.

"At Al Faktum."

"Oh, nobody in particular."

"You mean they're political detainees," Lorimer said.

"If you like."

"You approve of people being locked up for their political opinions? That makes them nobodies?"

"There are a great many things I don't approve of," Hassan retorted harshly. "One of them is moral superiority."

"Sorry," Lorimer said. "But surely the prison's important if O'Brien was killed because he'd been hanging about the place taking photographs?"

"I doubt if he was taking photographs," Hassan replied with a return to his former manner. "As you said, it was nearly dark."

"And as you said, he could have been using special film."

"Possibly."

"Anyway, if it was so dark, how did they recognize him? It could have been anybody out there."

"The police traced his car. He'd hired it at the airport when he and his wife arrived."

"I thought you said he'd hidden it in the dunes? How could they trace a car they hadn't seen?"

Their eyes met, and Hassan smiled. It was a thin smile, with as much warmth as the blade of a headsman's sword.

"He was framed," Lorimer said angrily. "I don't know why, I suppose your government wanted him out of the country, but it's obvious. If there was a car, it wasn't his. Probably there wasn't a car at all."

"You can take my word for it, there was, and it was his. It's been examined by our forensic experts. They could tell by sand and the other traces they found in it that it had been parked out in those dunes very recently. Tyre tracks there fitted the tyres on his car." Hassan paused. "There was another man there that night."

"Where?"

"One of the guards saw him running up the road towards O'Brien. They disappeared into the dunes together."

"How can you believe him?" Lorimer demanded. "They lied about O'Brien taking photographs, and probably about other things too."

"I trust him." Something in Hassan's tone, a slight emphasis on "him," told Lorimer that the guard was one of his men.

"If so, he must have come from the camp," he said. "You say it's over sixty miles out in the desert; nobody would set out to walk that far hoping for a lift."

"He could have gone with O'Brien, or by himself in another car."

"Was there one?"

"Not that I know of."

"O'Brien wouldn't have taken him. If he was spying on the camp, having anybody with him would make it more likely he was spotted."

Hassan nodded. "That's what I think. The chances are he came from the camp."

"But nobody will say he did?"

"No. Two days ago a man's body was washed up on the beach not far from the headland where O'Brien was found. According to his passport, his name was Sullivan and he came from Belfast. The doctors say he'd been in the water two or three days."

"You believe he was the man from the camp?" Lorimer asked.

"I don't know. There are a lot of things I don't know. I just wonder."

Lorimer frowned. "Was Sullivan drowned?" he asked.

Hassan gave him a level stare, as though half his mind was thinking about something else. "No," he answered. "His skull was smashed in and his body put in the sea."

There was a silence, broken when Mrs. Hassan came to tell them that dinner was ready.

It was a relaxed meal. Hassan appeared to have put his preoccupation with O'Brien aside for the time being, and he proved a friendly, courteous host. Rather to his surprise, Lorimer found he was enjoying himself. Until now Hassan had struck him as an unusually self-contained man, but in his wife's presence he became less reserved. Lorimer reflected that thirty-six hours ago he had been in London anticipating an unpleasant, possibly difficult two or three days looking into things at Maxwells' office and arranging for O'Brien's body to be flown home. So far his trip had been difficult in a wholly unexpected way. He had been shot at, questioned by the police twice, heard suggestions that O'Brien was some sort of spy, and now he was having dinner in their home with a Shajihan police inspector and his wife.

The Hassans had two sons, of twelve and nine, who were staying with Hassan's sister and her husband forty miles away.

"It's so quiet when they aren't here," Mary Hassan observed half-regretfully.

"Peaceful," her husband amended.

She laughed. "Did Ahmad tell you he was brought up in England?"

"No," Lorimer said.

She glanced at Hassan as if seeking his consent before she went on. "His father was the best-known newspaper editor in Shajiha. He was very respected, but he was always in trouble with the old regime, and in the end he had to leave the country. He went to Britain and worked for the BBC World Service, or whatever it was called then. Ahmad was only three when they went, and he lived in England until he was twenty-six. He went to Cambridge; then, after he graduated, he got a research post there. That's where I met him. He was so very English then." She laughed, eyeing her husband fondly.

"You British don't understand what it's like to be a refugee in another country," Hassan said. "Not knowing where your future will be. If you are young, you try to camouflage yourself so that you don't stand out amongst your friends, and hope they'll forget you're different. When I first came back, it was like coming to a foreign country. . . . I didn't realize how Anglicized I had become. I couldn't remember anything about Shajiha except what I had read and what my father had told me, and I had half-forgotten my own language."

"I wondered how you came to speak such perfect English," Lorimer said.

"We usually speak English at home."

"Four months after we met, the revolution happened and Ahmad decided he must come back," Mary went on. "That's why we got married in a hurry, not for the reason my friends thought. I wanted to be with him when he arrived, to be part of it all."

"Did your father come too?" Lorimer asked Hassan.

"No, he'd died a few months before. My mother had been dead nearly ten years."

"We don't keep in touch with people in England as much as we should," Mary said. "My family—and I write to one or two friends sometimes, and send cards at Christmas. You know how it is. We go back for holidays every year or two, and Ahmad goes to see his old tutor at Cambridge. You write to each other, too, don't you, darling?"

"Humphrey Downing," Hassan said with a smile.

"He thinks the world of Ahmad." Mary laughed. "I'm talking too much. I must go and see to the coffee."

"You said the police traced O'Brien's car," Lorimer said when she had gone. "As if you weren't one of them."

"It was a different division, that's all," Hassan told him.

"I don't believe you're an ordinary policeman."

"Which of us considers himself ordinary? To ourselves we are all extraordinary. Unique." Hassan smiled and leaned back in his chair, looking very much at his ease.

"How long is it since you did routine traffic work? Or handled an ordinary CID case?"

Lorimer hadn't expected his host to answer, and he wasn't surprised when Hassan changed the subject. "There won't be any problem about Mrs. O'Brien having her husband's body flown home," he said.

"You won't need it while you carry out your investigations?"

"There won't be any further investigation."

"*What?* He was murdered."

"Perhaps. Officially he committed suicide. The file has been closed."

"And that's good enough for you?"

"I have nothing to do with it. I told you, it isn't my case."

"Whose is it then?"

"Inspector Mahfuz's."

"And he's satisfied? Christ!"

"Don't underestimate him," Hassan said. "He's very intelligent—

and very efficient." It was clear from his tone he disliked his colleague; he made "efficient" sound like "unscrupulous." "Will you tell Mrs. O'Brien what you've learned today?"

"I don't know."

"What good would it do?"

This time it was Lorimer's turn not to answer. He was thinking that once O'Brien's body was back in England, a coroner could order a post-mortem and hold an inquest. It had happened in other cases. If he did, it would come out that O'Brien had been murdered, the Press could be relied on to take up the story, and the Foreign Office would probably be dragged into it. Mahfuz wouldn't be able to sweep it all under the carpet if that happened, closed file or not. But he had no intention of telling Hassan what he was thinking; if the Shajihan knew, he might well stop the body's leaving the country.

"I'll ask you one thing," Hassan said. "If you tell her, don't do it until you're both back in England. Please. Telling her before would make things very difficult."

"For you?" Lorimer asked.

"Yes."

"All right, I won't."

"Thank you, Graham."

The door opened and Mary Hassan came in carrying a tray loaded with coffee things. "You both look very serious," she said.

"I want a list of all Maxwells' ships that have docked here during the last two years," Lorimer told Oldfield brusquely. He was irritated by the manager's spinelessness, and he had a headache. "The dates they were here, where they came from, and where they were going to." An idea was taking shape in his mind.

Oldfield looked resentful. "I don't know," he said. "Some of the records have probably been destroyed by now. We clear out the old bumf when it's not going to be wanted any more."

Lorimer knew he was making difficulties in revenge for his curtness to him. Oldfield was as soft as a five-year-old girl. "It is wanted," he said bitingly. "Now."

The manager weakened. "It may take some time," he muttered.

"Then you'd better get on with it."

When Oldfield had gone, Lorimer sat staring at the desk in front of him. He was convinced that Hassan knew—or, at least, strongly suspected—what was going on. He had told him far more than he had had any right to expect: about the camp at Al Faktum, for one thing. What the hell had O'Brien thought he was doing, hanging about round a camp for political prisoners in a country like this? He must have been mad.

Or a bloody Scarlet Pimpernel. The idea was too way out, too fantastic, he thought. But no more fantastic than the notion of O'Brien as a spy.

God knew what Grantley would say. For the second time Lorimer wondered whether the Chairman had known O'Brien was up to something out here and had sent him out as a sort of stalking lamb, to see what reaction he would stir up.

Why pick him? Lorimer knew the answer to that, in perhaps his one candid moment Grantley had told him: He could be spared. No doubt Rayment had suggested him for the job. Borrett didn't like him; Borrett wanted a PA who would bolster his ego and make a great show of doing nothing just as he did, and he would have passed on his feelings to Rayment. Sod them all. His headache was fading, and Lorimer grinned.

Going out to the main office, he collected some of the books he had examined the day before and carried them back to Oldfield's room. Perhaps now he knew a little more, they would tell him something he had missed yesterday, but he had no great hopes.

It was some time before Oldfield came in with a sheet of paper in his hand.

"The *Maxwell Pride*'s called here nine times," he reported. "The *Maxwell Glory*'s been twice and the *Maxwell Triumph* once."

"What were they carrying?" Lorimer asked.

"Just ordinary general cargo."

"I want to know what it was."

"It wasn't anything special."

"Just let me know what."

"Very well." Oldfield assumed a long-suffering expression.

"And who it was shipped by, and who to. Coming into the country and going out," Lorimer added brutally. It was unlikely he would learn anything useful from the exercise, but he had better check the cargoes, just in case.

The manager put the sheet of paper on the desk and went out looking aggrieved. Lorimer guessed he had hoped for praise for producing the information about the sailings so promptly despite his gloomy forebodings. He wouldn't get it. Hell, Oldfield wasn't a junior clerk, he was supposed to be in charge here.

Lorimer looked at the list. Neither of the other ships had called at Dhartoum for over a year, but the *Maxwell Pride* had been here for two days only last week, sailing for Piraeus the day after O'Brien was killed. The previous day Lorimer had made a note of O'Brien's visits; he took out the list now and compared the dates with those of the ships' calls. Neither the *Maxwell Glory* nor the *Maxwell Triumph* had been in Dhartoum while O'Brien was here, but six of the *Maxwell Pride*'s nine calls had corresponded with his visits. To put it another way, every time O'Brien came to Dhartoum, the *Maxwell Pride* did, too. Was that coincidence, or had it some more sinister significance?

Through the thin connecting door Lorimer could hear the sounds of work from the outer office, the occasional tinkle of a phone, the light thud of electric typewriters, snatches of talk. What had O'Brien done on his too-frequent visits?

Lorimer was pretty sure Hassan believed he had been smuggling escaped political prisoners out of the country, and powerful men like Saad Hatem's backers had found out and murdered him, staging a fake suicide, because they couldn't bring him to trial.

Where did Hassan himself stand? Lorimer took it for granted he was a member of the security police, or whatever the Shajihan equivalent of the Special Branch called itself. He hadn't arrested O'Brien, presumably the latter's death had come too soon, but why had he told him, Lorimer, that O'Brien was murdered? If he had said nothing, the truth would never have been known to anyone outside a small group here. He must have had some motive, he wasn't a man to act without a reason. Was he involved in the same enterprise as O'Brien, or was he out to smash the power of men who took the law into their own hands, acting as judge, jury and executioner? Lorimer thought the second was far more likely.

And now? Last night he had promised Hassan he would say nothing to Janet until they were back in Britain. He must tell her then, she had a right to know her husband hadn't committed suicide, but perhaps Hassan was right and it would achieve nothing. Even if a coroner did order an inquest and ruled that O'Brien was murdered, what good would it do? The Foreign Office might make approaches to the Shajihan government, but they were unlikely to receive any response more positive than a diplomatic shrug of the shoulders, and the matter would be allowed to die. Nobody would be interested enough to do any more.

So why should he be? He hadn't known O'Brien, who seemed to have been either a romantic fool or a paid mercenary. Either way, he had asked for trouble. It was fortunate the authorities here appeared to accept that he had been acting on his own, without his company's knowledge, and Maxwells wouldn't suffer because of him. At least he would have that to tell Grantley.

Another possibility occurred to him: Had Oldfield known anything about O'Brien's activities? If he had, it would explain his reluctance to provide any information that might shed a light on them. Lorimer went to the door and called him.

The manager came in looking worried. But that was only his normal nervousness, it didn't take lengthy or subtle questioning to satisfy Lorimer O'Brien had told him nothing.' He wasn't surprised— Oldfield looked incapable of keeping any secret if the slightest pressure was put on him.

"Had he any friends out here?" Lorimer persisted. "Any people he saw regularly?"

As far as Oldfield knew, there was nobody. O'Brien had maintained the usual contacts in government departments and among the business community, but there was nothing suspicious about that. Unless . . . He could hardly have organized the actual escapes from the prison at Al Faktum, there must have been at least one other person involved, and probably several. Possibly one of them inside the camp. Had one of O'Brien's contacts in a ministry been part of the operation? If so, he—or she—would have had a great deal to lose. Had they learned O'Brien was suspected, and killed him to prevent his talking?

Lorimer picked up Oldfield's list again. But although he stared at it for several minutes, it told him nothing new. The only factor common to all the *Maxwell Pride*'s voyages was Marseilles; she always called there on her way back to her home port in Britain from Dhartoum. Was that significant? Marseilles was a tough city with a large underworld; an escaped prisoner might go to ground there, perhaps to emerge later with a new appearance and new papers, almost a new identity. And there the trail would end.

Not that that mattered as far as he was concerned; it wasn't part of his job to trace the prisoners. For that matter, it wasn't up to him to discover what had happened to O'Brien either. Or why. His instructions were to see O'Brien's death meant no problems for the Group, to arrange for his body to be flown back to Britain, and to escort Mrs. O'Brien home. It had sounded simple.

If a hired gunman hadn't tried to kill him, and Hassan hadn't told him that O'Brien was murdered, it would have been simple, too.

The phone beside the bed rang. As Lorimer walked across the room to answer it, he noticed that the clock on the bedside table said six minutes past seven; in a few minutes he would go down to the bar for a drink. He would take his time over it, and when he had finished it he would stroll in to dinner. Already, after two days here, he was taking life at a more leisurely pace.

"Lorimer," he said.

"There is a call for you, sir," the operator told him. She had a pretty accent and sounded like a pretty girl.

Lorimer told himself that voices were as deceptive as first impressions; she was probably fifty and as ugly as the sculpture in the hotel lobby. "Thank you," he said.

There was a click. Then, "Graham? This is Mary Hassan."

Voices weren't always misleading, he could tell she had been crying.

"Hallo, Mary," he said. "Is something wrong?"

"Are you alone?"

"Yes."

"Ahmad's dead."

Lorimer could hear the shocked disbelief, the grief and the emptiness in her voice. He was shocked himself. "Oh my God!" he said. "When? What happened?"

"This morning, when he was going to work. They killed him."

The impersonal neatness of his room seemed to impress itself on Lorimer's mind as if to insulate him from thinking about Hassan. For the first time he consciously noticed the pattern of the carpet and the way the curtains were hung.

"There was a bomb under his car," Mary said. She was crying again, he could hear the tears even over the phone. "Oh God, Graham! I'm so bloody angry."

He guessed she didn't swear often and it made her words even more shocking.

"Who did it?" he asked. "Do they know?"

"No."

"Where are you now?"

"At our neighbours'. They've been very kind, and I thought it would be better if I didn't ring from home, just in case."

"Is there anything I can do?"

"No. But thank you for asking. I'm sorry to bother you, but I—I wanted you to know."

"I'm glad you did," Lorimer told her. "And you haven't bothered me." He paused. "Mary, who did he work for?"

"He was an Inspector in the Security Police. I thought you knew. He was sure there was something serious going on. Did he tell you?"

"Part of it."

"That's really why he asked you to dinner last night. He'd never done that with British people out here before, except one or two friends like Humphrey Downing. He trusted you."

"I couldn't help him much." It sounded like an admission of betrayal, Lorimer thought. But it was true, he hadn't kept anything back except his curiosity about O'Brien's frequent trips to Dhartoum, and that wouldn't have told Hassan anything he didn't already know. "Did he ever talk about what he thought was going on?" he asked.

"Not really. He didn't tell me much about his work, most of it was secret." Mary hesitated. "I must go. You didn't mind my ringing, did you?"

"No, of course not," Lorimer told her. "If there is anything I can do, or if you want me for anything, I shan't be leaving until the day after tomorrow."

"Thank you, Graham. I'm glad Ahmad brought you last night, we both enjoyed the evening." Mary's voice broke. "Goodbye."

"Goodbye, Mary," Lorimer said. "I'm very sorry."

He meant it, he thought, putting down the phone. He had hardly known Hassan, and their relationship had initially been that of policeman and potential suspect, hardly the most favourable basis for friendship, yet now he felt a genuine sorrow. He told himself it was the shock, perhaps even the realization that it might have been he who died instead of Hassan, but he knew that was only a small part of it. There had been an integrity in the Shajihan, and last night, when he was at home with his wife, he had revealed a more human side. That he and Mary were devoted to each other was obvious.

Lorimer was glad there was no one to mourn like that if he died. Rosalind would be sorry, she would probably cry a little at first, but they had made the break and she wouldn't feel a great sense of loss.

Mary Hassan and Janet O'Brien must be roughly the same age, and both of them had two children. Three lives at least had been devastated as a result of O'Brien's illegal activities, possibly six; Lorimer suspected that Hassan, too, had been murdered because he knew too much about the escape organization. Whatever his intentions, whether he had acted from some quixotic motive or for money, had any man the right to cause so much misery?

O'Brien's coffin had already been loaded into the cargo hold of the airbus out on the tarmac. Janet was relieved that she wouldn't have to see it, the knowledge that it was there aboard the plane in which very soon she would be flying home was bad enough. Graham had been very good; he had seen to everything, dealing with officials and taking all the responsibilities off her shoulders. If only he could have taken this feeling of guilt, too. . . . .

It wasn't fair she should feel guilty. After all, it wasn't her fault she and Mike had drifted apart these last few years; it was just one of those things, it happened to lots of couples who had been married a long time. But now she was ashamed because she didn't feel more stricken with grief. She was sad and outraged, but that was all. If only she could really grieve, it would salve her conscience.

But it wouldn't lessen her fear.

Mahfuz had come to see them off, looking larger than ever in uniform. Lorimer wondered why he was there, and supposed the Inspector wanted to satisfy himself they left the country. That suggested he knew what O'Brien had been doing and suspected he was involved also. Lorimer remembered what Hassan had said about Mahfuz's efficiency, and that he shouldn't be underestimated.

Thinking about it now with the benefit of hindsight, it was strange that Mahfuz hadn't done more to see whether he could identify the gunman in the Mercedes. Perhaps, as Hassan had said, the civil police were overworked and he had been ready to take the easy line that the shooting was just one more incident in the taxi war. He might even believe it.

He was leaning towards Janet now, his manner a blend of deference and concern that seemed to Lorimer somehow vaguely unpleasant.

"I hope you will have as pleasing a journey as possible in the sad circumstances, Mrs. O'Brien," he told her. "Shajihan National Airlines are famous for their service, and I am sure they will care for you well."

For a moment Lorimer thought the big man was about to kiss Janet's hand and wondered how she would react if he did, but Mahfuz didn't. Instead he glanced across at Lorimer, an unfathomable expression in his eyes.

"You will be glad to be home again, no doubt, Mr. Lorimer," he said.

"Yes," Lorimer agreed. "I will."

A minute later their flight was called.

"Inspector Mahfuz has been very kind," Janet remarked when she and Lorimer were settled in their seats.

Because she hated flying, and looking out made her feel worse, she had asked him to take the window seat. He looked out now and saw Mahfuz standing at a window of the departure lounge watching the plane. Or was he watching them? he wondered.

The airbus began taxiing towards the runway and the Inspector disappeared from sight.

EIGHT

"Sit down," Grantley said. Lorimer obeyed. "Well?"

"You said you wanted me to report to you when I got back, sir."

"I did. What have you got to tell me?"

Lorimer eyed the Chairman sitting back in his big swivel chair, hunched and alert. "I'd like to know why you picked me to go out there," he said.

Grantley's expression didn't change. "I told you why."

"You said I could be spared. Was that the only reason?"

There was a momentary pause before Grantley asked, "Does it make any difference?"

"Ay, it does. I'd like to know. I was shot at and nearly killed within an hour of my getting there. The man driving my taxi was hit. I didn't know it was going to be that sort of trip."

The Chairman leaned forward and his eyes met Lorimer's unwaveringly. "You were what?" he demanded.

Lorimer told him.

This time the pause before Grantley spoke was longer. "Are you making this up?" he asked.

"No, sir."

"Why should anyone out there want to kill you? He must have been shooting at somebody else, the taxi-driver most likely."

"No. The Security Police out there know it was me. He picked me out at the airport." The Old Man wasn't going to like this, Lorimer thought. "O'Brien didn't kill himself, he was murdered," he said.

Grantley didn't like it. Nor was he prepared to believe it just because Lorimer said so. "Have you any grounds for saying that?" he demanded.

"Plenty. Maxwells' manager out there is a man named Oldfield. He says O'Brien was looking forward to coming home; he had something on his mind, but he wasn't depressed. Second, he didn't leave a note or give any hint of what he was going to do."

"Suicides don't always."

"They don't hit themselves hard on the back of the head before they fix a pipe to the exhaust, either," Lorimer said. "Not hard enough to dent their skulls."

Grantley wondered if he had made a mistake sending Lorimer out to Dhartoum. Did he harbour an over-vivid Celtic imagination under his dour exterior? The Scottish mind had more labyrinths than most. If so, there was still time to put things right. "What does Mrs. O'Brien say?" he asked.

"That her husband was depressed. The job was getting on top of him because people had let him down."

"She should know better than the manager."

"If she's telling the truth."

"Why shouldn't she be?"

"She's frightened. I don't know what of. And it wasn't my idea he was murdered, it was an Inspector's in the Security Police, Hassan. He took me to see O'Brien's body at the mortuary, and showed me the injury to his skull."

"You seem to have had an unpleasant trip," Grantley observed. "I'm sorry. Was O'Brien robbed?"

"No."

"How did you come to be mixed up with the Security Police?"

"For the same reason I think I was shot at; people out there thought I had come to take over O'Brien's job." Lorimer paused. This was something else the Chairman wouldn't like. "He was smuggling escaped political prisoners out of Shajiha."

Grantley was hardened to disturbing news, but now he was shocked as well as startled. "He was *what?*" he demanded.

"There's a prison camp a hundred miles out in the desert; he was spotted hanging about there the night before he was killed. He'd left his car hidden in some sandhills, and one of the guards saw another man going up the road from the camp towards him. They ran to the car, and it looks as if O'Brien drove the other man back to Dhartoum. A couple of days later a man's body was washed up near the headland where O'Brien was found. The police believe he was the man O'Brien picked up at the camp. O'Brien had been out to Dhartoum six times in less than two years. Why? It's only a small branch, mostly it handles deliveries for Group companies to customers out there and general cargo back. And every time he went to Dhartoum, one of Maxwells' ships, the *Maxwell Pride*, called there."

"What has that got to do with it?" Grantley demanded. He didn't like the sound of this, and he was more than half-convinced he had to take Lorimer seriously.

"I don't know," the Scot admitted. "The trouble is it all hangs together, and it makes a sort of pattern. Hassan believed O'Brien was involved in some organization to get prisoners out of the country, and he was no fool."

If the Shajihan police found proof of O'Brien's being mixed up in such a lunatic scheme, God knew what the result would be for Maxwells, Grantley thought. And indirectly for United. It was the sort of trouble he wanted to avoid at all costs. Hopefully the worst wouldn't happen, and no proof would be found. Then the whole business would fade like a mirage in the desert. Perhaps, despite all Lorimer's arguments, that was all it was. But Grantley wasn't a man to postpone consideration of action because the trouble might never materialize.

"What's Hassan going to do about it?" he asked.

"Nothing," Lorimer replied.

"Nothing?"

"He was murdered three days ago. Somebody put a bomb under his car."

"Good God!"

"He told me the man who shot at me had powerful friends."

For a moment the Chairman said nothing, then he asked, "How much of all this does Mrs. O'Brien know?"

"Nothing, unless her husband told her what he was doing. Perhaps he did, and that's why she's scared. I haven't said anything." Lorimer hesitated. "She says he claimed people had let him down. She thinks he meant people he dealt with in his work for Maxwells, but it could have been something to do with his driving out to the camp that night. Anyway, she's adamant that he committed suicide."

A telephone on the Chairman's desk rang and he picked it up.

"The Minister of Trade and Industry would like to speak to you, Sir Aidan," Mrs. Wilkins said.

"Not now, Helen. Ask if I can ring him back." Grantley replaced the phone. "Did you bring O'Brien's body back with you?" he asked Lorimer.

"Yes. The cremation's fixed for Thursday, but if the coroner ordered a post-mortem, the pathologist would find the damage to the skull and there'd have to be an inquest. That would mean postponing the cremation."

"And that's what you want? What do you think it would achieve, apart from a lot of rumours, stories in the papers, and Mrs. O'Brien's being hounded by the police and the Press?" And United dragged into it, Grantley thought. For nothing.

"The truth?" Lorimer suggested. But who cared about such abstracts? He wasn't certain he saw simply knowing the truth as a very high priority himself. Sometimes it was a little too much like voyeurism. "At least she would know he didn't kill himself," he said. "And she might get more money from the insurance companies."

That was the only aspect that really concerned Grantley, and United could take care of it and make sure she didn't lose.

"You say she's accepted the idea of suicide," he pointed out. "Do you think it would help her to have it all raked up, probably for nothing?" He walked to the nearer of the big windows and looked out. Not for the first time when he was standing there he recalled the scene in *The Third Man* where Harry Lime looks down from the giant wheel in the amusement park and asks Martins to say honestly if he would feel anything if one of those tiny dots far below stopped moving. It wasn't a sense of omniscience looking down from such a height gave you, he reflected, it was remoteness from other men. Yet such detachment was necessary sometimes when painful decisions had to be taken.

"Bury it," he said over his shoulder. "We have too many interests out there, we can't afford to create bad feeling for nothing. If you're right about O'Brien, it may well have been somebody working for their police or government who killed him. For reasons of their own they didn't want a trial, so they dealt with him that way." He turned.

"You want me to forget it," Lorimer said.

"I don't expect you to like it, but think of all the British people who live out there," Grantley told him, harshness returning to his voice. "And the jobs that would go here if we lost that market."

There didn't seem any adequate answer to that, Lorimer thought.

Nevertheless, he wasn't satisfied. Men like Grantley could always justify the course they wanted to follow, it was part of their stock-in-trade.

"What do I do now?" he asked.

"Represent United at O'Brien's funeral. Apart from that, nothing. Take the rest of the week off, you've earned a break."

Lorimer didn't want a holiday, but it seemed impolitic to say so. So he said simply, "Thank you, sir."

"Give Philip Rayment a ring on Monday," the Chairman told him.

"Right, sir." Lorimer wondered why he should call the Personnel Director, but he didn't ask; sufficient unto the day, he thought, walking to the door.

"Thank you, Lorimer," Grantley said. "I'm sorry you had such an exciting time."

Sarcastic bastard! Lorimer thought, going out. As he passed her desk, Helen Wilkins looked up and smiled brightly.

"Did you have a good trip?" she asked.

"It could have been worse," Lorimer answered.

"Oh well." For Grantley's secretary the meaningless phrase covered a wide range of possibilities and uncertainties, she used it all the time.

Lorimer crossed the landing to the lift, got in and pressed the button for the ground floor. He wished he hadn't so many reservations about the Shajiha business. Especially about Janet O'Brien.

Outside in the street, it was grey and drizzling, and although it wasn't cold, he shivered. After only a few days in Dhartoum he had become accustomed to feeling hot. Here in London people seemed to be walking faster than usual to reach their destinations as quickly as they could in order to escape from the weather. Others, coming out of shops and offices, lingered in doorways before braving it. A flag on a building opposite hung limp against its mast. Lorimer drew a deep breath. In spite of the exhaust fumes and the odour of cooking from an Indian restaurant a few doors away, he relished the mild, damp air.

There were several people waiting at the bus-stop across the street. Among them was a slight young man with a darkish complexion wearing a navy-blue anorak. Lorimer noticed him, then a bus coming from Victoria pulled up at the stop and he was hidden.

Some impulse made Lorimer step back into the lobby, where the tinted glass formed a bastion against prying eyes. After a minute the bus moved off, but the young man remained, alone at the stop. His right hand, thrust deep into the pocket of his anorak, made it bulge, as if he were holding something heavy there. He was staring straight across the street, and although he knew he couldn't see him, Lorimer felt exposed. Why should he think the young man was looking for him? He was glancing to his left and right now, seemingly searching for someone in the throng of people on this side of the street. Apparently he didn't see anyone, for after a moment's hesitation he started walking towards the station, to be swallowed up almost at once in the crowd.

There was no reason why he should have noticed him particularly, Lorimer thought. Except that he had seemed to be watching the United Building. And that he was almost certainly an Arab.

He walked out through the swing doors and set off in the opposite direction, towards Westminster.

That afternoon, disregarding Grantley's instructions to forget all that had happened, Lorimer drove out to Surrey to see Janet O'Brien.

The Overseas Manager's home was a largish 1930s house in a big garden. It was partly screened from the road by a beech hedge, and at one side there was a fairly new brick-built double garage. In the warm, damp weather of the past week, the lawn had grown two or three inches, giving the house a slightly neglected appearance.

Lorimer skirted the orange Mini parked in front of the garage and tugged the wrought-iron bell in the porch. The bell clanged unmusically somewhere in the house and he waited, looking round with interest. After the morning's drizzle it was a beautiful afternoon, but the bright sunshine seemed to accentuate the faint air of neglect rather than diminish it. A bicycle leaned at a precarious angle against the garage wall, its front wheel turned outwards, as if its rider had dismounted and thrown it there in his haste.

Janet opened the door wearing a blue-check shirt and bright-blue trousers that stretched tight over her ample hips. She still looked strained, but less shocked than the last time he saw her, Lorimer thought.

"Graham!" she exclaimed. "This is a nice surprise. Come in."

He followed her across a narrow hall and into a pleasant room made half-dark by its leaded windows and a large sycamore growing close to the house. She was nervous, he thought. It showed in the quick way she spoke, and her restlessness. She was fidgeting now, her fingers worrying the arms of her chair.

"How are you?" he asked.

"Oh, you know." She spoke brightly, but although she smiled, her eyes didn't meet his.

"How have your children taken it?"

"They're upset. Of course they are; Juliet thought the world of her father. And Stephen too."

Lorimer noticed the distinction she made between the children, and her attempt to cover it up. She had looked away, too.

"What are you frightened of?" he asked quietly.

She faced him then, for a moment. But after a second or two she looked down at her hands, twisting in her lap now. "Frightened?" she countered, her voice pitched a little higher. "Why should I be frightened?"

"I don't know, but anybody can see you're scared of something. It might help if you told me what it is."

"But I'm not!"

"All right." Lorimer reckoned there was nothing to be gained by pressing her. More than likely she would tell him soon, anyway; it took a stronger will than Janet's to keep secret something that was bothering her so much. Or real fear of the consequences of talking about it.

She stood up and walked to the mantelpiece. A packet of cigarettes was lying there and she picked it up, making rather a deal of extracting one and putting it between her lips because her hands were shaking.

"I'm sorry; will you?" She held out the packet to him.

"I don't smoke. I didn't think you did, either." She had told him she didn't when he asked if she wanted their seats on the plane in the smoking or non-smoking sections.

"I don't much." She sat down again, perching near the edge of her chair and putting the packet on the coffee-table beside her. "Why do you say I'm frightened?" It was like an aching tooth, she couldn't leave it alone.

Lorimer waited until she had to look at him, but he still didn't answer her question. Instead he said, "The night before he died, your husband drove a hundred miles out into the desert. Did he tell you where he went?"

"No." Janet's reply was barely audible.

"What did he say when he got back?"

"Does it matter?"

"Very much," Lorimer told her roughly. Janet was beginning to annoy him.

"He said it was all a shambles."

"What was?"

"I don't know. I didn't take much notice, he often used to get angry about things. He seemed to think he'd been made a fool of somehow." Janet stubbed out her cigarette.

"How?"

"I've no idea."

Again Lorimer waited. "He didn't commit suicide," he said at last. "He was murdered. He was angry, not depressed. Angry because he'd been used and let down. You've known all along, haven't you? That's why you're frightened. What is it you know, Janet?"

"I don't know anything," she cried, distraught. "What is it? You weren't like this in Dhartoum. Mike's dead, why can't you leave it alone?"

"Because he was murdered and they killed a man I knew and liked. They tried to kill me. Don't you see, once you've said what it is, there won't be anything more for you to be scared of."

He shouldn't have told her that, Lorimer thought. It wasn't true. Saad Hatem's friends would kill her as ruthlessly as they had the others, whether it was to protect themselves or in retribution if she talked. Ironically, that was why she must.

"All right, if you don't want to tell me," he said.

"There isn't anything to tell you!"

As Janet spoke, the door opened and a youth of about seventeen and a girl two or three years younger came in. They stopped, looking from Janet to Lorimer. The boy was tall, with dark hair, arrogant eyes and too much flesh on his big-boned frame. It showed round his sullen, spoilt mouth and his waist and hips. The girl was dark, too, but slender, with a child's skinny arms protruding from the short sleeves of her shirt. She was wearing shabby fawn trousers and riding boots.

"Who's this?" the boy asked rudely, looking at Janet.

"Mr. Lorimer, Stephen. Don't you remember, I told you he came out to help me in Dhartoum?"

Lorimer thought she might have told him to mind his manners, too.

"What's he doing here?" Stephen demanded officiously.

"That's no business of yours, sonny," Lorimer told him.

The boy glared. "If you've been upsetting my mother . . ." he began.

"What makes you think I might have been? Or do you usually speak to her visitors like this?"

Stephen reddened.

"He hasn't upset me, darling," Janet said. It was clear she liked, perhaps was even a little thrilled by, her son's attitude. To her his rudeness seemed only protective.

"If you change your mind, or if there's anything I can do," Lorimer told her, ignoring Stephen, "you know where to get hold of me."

"Yes. Thank you, Graham." She managed a wan smile as she went out to the hall with him. "Thank you for coming," she said at the front door.

After the cool air indoors, it was very warm outside in the garden. Lorimer had parked his Saab in the road, and he started walking back down the drive. When he had gone halfway he heard footsteps hurrying behind him and stopped, turning. The girl was running after him.

"I'm Juliet O'Brien," she said, panting slightly. She had a pointed little face with frank grey eyes and freckles across her nose.

"I guessed you were." Lorimer wondered if he was about to be attacked a second time within five minutes. If so, he much preferred the look of this assailant.

"Do you mind if I speak to you?" Juliet asked. She looked unhappy and unsure of herself, but there was a diffident courage in the way she faced him.

"No, of course not," Lorimer told her.

"Do you know what really happened?"

"Hasn't your mother told you?"

"Not really. At least . . . Daddy didn't—he didn't kill himself, did he?"

"No." Lorimer felt a sudden bitter anger that Janet, because she was frightened, had burdened Juliet with the false belief that her father had committed suicide.

"She said he did."

"I don't think she knew for sure then."

"But if he didn't . . ." It was as though a whole new world of possibilities was opening up in front of Juliet, and as yet she couldn't really comprehend them. "It can't have been an accident, can it?"

"We don't know yet what really happened," Lorimer told her gently. "Only that he didn't kill himself."

"I would like to know." Juliet paused. "Stephen was very rude. He likes to think he's the man of the house now; he's Mother's favourite. She and Daddy were always arguing. I shouldn't tell you that, should I?"

"No," Lorimer agreed. "But it doesn't necessarily mean they didn't care for each other. People sometimes quarrel with people they love because they care so much about what they think." Listen to me, he thought. The great philosopher. I couldn't even keep my own wife from leaving me.

"They didn't love each other," Juliet said bitterly. "I don't think she cares Daddy's dead."

"You wouldn't say that if you'd seen her in Dhartoum. She was very upset." You bloody hypocrite, Lorimer thought. She was upset because she was scared.

But maybe that wasn't the whole truth, either.

Juliet looked up at him, her eyes solemn. "You didn't mind me speaking to you, did you?" she asked.

"Of course not. I'm glad you did."

"So am I." She gave him a sudden brilliant smile. "Goodbye, Mr. Lorimer."

"Goodbye, Juliet."

She watched him unlock his car door and slide in behind the wheel, and when he looked in the rear-view mirror before turning out into the main road she was still standing by the gate looking after him. Poor kid, he thought.

He hardly noticed the red Ford Sierra that pulled away from the kerb a couple of hundred yards farther down the side road. It came up to the Saab at the T-junction, and it was still there when he glanced in the mirror five minutes later, staying well back, allowing other vehicles to come between itself and the Turbo.

Three miles farther on, the Sierra was over a hundred yards in the rear, behind a Rover and a blue Datsun. Just ahead a road went off to the left, leading across-country to the A22. The Datsun turned onto it, but the Sierra remained. So it did at a big roundabout a mile farther on. Lorimer slowed. The Rover overtook him, the driver glancing across casually as it went past, but the Ford slowed too.

Lorimer wondered what the driver was planning. Before long they would be running into the first sprawling outer suburbs of London and heavier traffic.

Ahead of him were two large articulated lorries doing just under sixty miles an hour. He pressed his right foot down harder and the Saab surged forward. As soon as he was past the leading lorry, he pulled back sharply into the inside lane and slowed to the lorry's speed. Its driver flashed his headlights and hooted angrily.

"Sorry, Jimmy, but get lost," Lorimer muttered under his breath.

A moment later in his mirror he saw the Sierra passing the second lorry. Its driver, finding there was no room to pull in behind the Saab, had no alternative but to carry on in the outside lane. Lorimer smiled grimly.

He could see a sign for a "B" road turning off on the left. At the last moment, when the Sierra's driver was already committed to driving straight on, Lorimer turned the Saab's wheel to the left. The lorry had been too close for him to brake, and for several seconds the Turbo rocked alarmingly. Then it was heading fast for the hedge on the wrong side of the road. Lorimer heard another angry blast from the lorry's horn behind him. He braked. The car lurched rebelliously, then steadied as fifty yards ahead a tractor appeared suddenly round a bend. He braked harder, and the Saab, slowing, scraped past with inches to spare.

Lorimer smiled to himself. For someone who prided himself on driving sensibly, and with consideration for other people on the roads, that was a pretty fair example of behaving like an irresponsible bastard, he thought. Pulling into the side of the road, he took out his diary and made a note of the Sierra's number.

Lorimer picked up his camera, checked that the 135-millimeter lens was locked on, and walked through to his bedroom. It was eight o'clock and the young man was still there where he had been, with short breaks, for the last hour and a half, leaning against the wall near the entrance to the block of flats across the road. Lorimer suspected that during the breaks he had either gone to phone his report, or moved his vantage point a short distance along Southwold Terrace.

He could see him better from here than from the living room, a slight, dark man with narrow features and a thin, high-bridged nose. It was the same man he had seen at the bus-stop opposite United's offices this lunch-time. The man's face wasn't in the shadows as it had been when he first saw him. Apparently he didn't care if he was spotted, for he was making no attempt to keep out of sight. To Lorimer it seemed his confidence held a vague menace.

He raised his camera. As he did so the man turned, his attention caught by something farther along the road. Lorimer cursed. But a moment later the man turned back, and with a grunt of satisfaction Lorimer pressed the shutter-release button.

He took four shots, then, sitting on his bed, rewound the film into the cassette and extracted the cassette from the camera. He was slipping it into his pocket when the doorbell rang.

Melissa Forster was standing on the landing looking superb in white and black.

"I asked Dad and he said you were back," she said. "Aren't you going to ask me in?"

NINE

"Have a good trip?" Borrett inquired, glancing up from the *Financial Times* and holding it so that Lorimer wouldn't see he was reading the arts page. He might have very little interest in his assistant's activities, but he prided himself on observing the courtesies.

"All right, thanks." Lorimer regarded the heap of files on his desk with a sardonic eye. Everything had been left for his return, put out each morning to grow a little before it was locked away again in the evening. It was his work, and it would never have occurred to Borrett that he might do any of it.

"You might have a look at the letter from the Federation," he said now. "We shall have to answer it, I suppose. And draft something for me for the Board meeting this afternoon and let me have it, will you? Oh, and there was a message; Jim Forster wants to see you. I told him you wouldn't be back for a day or two." Borrett assumed a martyred expression. "We've been rushed off our feet while you were away."

Lorimer suppressed a smile. Having no need of a personal assistant, Borrett had so quickly accustomed himself to the luxury that now he felt ill-used if deprived of his services for even a few days.

"Sir Aidan told me to take the rest of the week off," he said.

"Oh, very well." Borrett looked resigned. "If he said so, I suppose you'd better."

"There are some things I still have to clear up, and he wants me to go to O'Brien's funeral."

Borrett could hardly complain about that, Lorimer thought. He supposed Forster wanted a report, and wondered whether Maxwells' Managing Director knew that Melissa had been to see him last night. "I'll give Mr. Forster's secretary a ring and see when he wants to see me," he said.

Borrett nodded. He suspected that his PA's being picked to go out to Shajiha indicated one of two things, both unwelcome: that Philip Rayment reckoned Lorimer could more easily be spared than anyone else of his rank, or that he wouldn't be with him much longer. The second meant at best his having to train a new assistant, at worst that Lorimer wouldn't be replaced. Borrett had no illusions about his standing in the eyes of the top floor.

Lorimer returned to the cubby-hole that was his office, rang Forster's secretary, and after a brief wait was told that Mr. Forster would see him right away.

Maxwells' chief executive was sitting at his desk when he was shown in. He didn't stand up or hold out his hand, and his nod was brusque. Lorimer scented trouble, and wondered what he had done.

"You wanted to see me, Mr. Forster?" he said.

"Yes, I did." Forster didn't suggest he sit down; he was angry and he intended Lorimer to see it. His tone was as curt as his nod had been, and he waited for at least a quarter of a minute, leaning forward, his forearms on his desk, the muscles of his face tense and his eyes hard, before he said, "I suppose you think that because for the time being you're working for the Chairman, that gives you the right to do what you like. Well, you can take it from me it doesn't. I may not be able to deal with you myself as I would if you were on Maxwells' staff, but it doesn't prevent me telling you what I think of your behaviour. Or letting the Chairman know."

Lorimer was taken aback. What the hell was Forster on about? He was angry, too, and as usual when he was roused, the Scots in his speech became more marked. "I beg your pardon?" he said softly. It sounded more like a warning than an apology.

"I don't know why Sir Aidan chose you to go out to Dhartoum instead of leaving it to us to send somebody from Maxwells," Forster told him. "I don't care about that; he's the Chairman, and no doubt he had his reasons. What I will not have is your going behind my back and upsetting Mrs. O'Brien with ludicrous stories about her husband being murdered. What right did you think you had? Hadn't she suffered enough already?"

"You think she'd rather believe he killed himself?" Lorimer asked, controlling his anger. "And it wasn't my idea he was murdered."

"Whose was it then?"

"Inspector Hassan's. O'Brien was hit on the head before he was put in his car. His skull was fractured."

Forster's expression didn't change. "Who's Hassan? I thought the man in charge was"—he glanced down at a pad on his desk—"an Inspector Mahfuz."

"Hassan was in the Security Police," Lorimer said.

Forster frowned. "Why should their Security Police be interested in what happened to O'Brien?"

"They seemed to think he was killed because he was mixed up in something illegal out there."

"What sort of thing?"

"Smuggling."

Forster's look blended dislike with incredulity. "Mike O'Brien?" he said. "You don't know what you're talking about; he was the last man to get involved in anything like that. If you're naive enough to take notice of every malicious rumour you hear, you won't go far with United."

"I said, that's what the Security Police thought," Lorimer told him.

"Meaning you don't?"

"He may have been. It was his sixth trip to Dhartoum in less than two years. Why did he go so often?"

"I've no idea," Forster answered coldly. "He was a good man at his job, I didn't tell him how to do it."

Lorimer saw no reason to tell Forster everything. He had reported to Grantley and been told to forget all about O'Brien's probable activities. No doubt Forster's response would be the same. Moreover he suspected that the main thrust of Forster's attack had been blunted, and he was no longer so sure of his ground. He had been pushed into taking the position he had, and Lorimer was pretty sure he knew who had done the pushing. But there was more to it than that; for some reason Forster had welcomed the opportunity to bawl him out.

"Sir Aidan told me it was part of my job to make sure there was nothing wrong out there that might affect Maxwells," he said. "If Hassan was right, and it came out, they would be involved, even if nobody in the company knew what O'Brien was doing. It could make a lot of trouble for them."

"That's no excuse for your upsetting Mrs. O'Brien," Forster persisted grimly.

"Who told you I upset her? Did she?"

"Her son says he came home and found you just leaving. She was very distressed and at first she wouldn't tell him what you'd said, but he persuaded her."

Lorimer suspected that Stephen O'Brien had been less concerned with protecting his mother than with promoting his own image as the man of the family, but he didn't say so. "I didn't have to tell her O'Brien was murdered," he said. "She knew. That's why she's so scared."

Forster leaned back in his chair. "You were sent out to Dhartoum to finish off any work Mike O'Brien had left and help Mrs. O'Brien," he said harshly. "It seems you went a long way beyond what you were told to do, and as a result Maxwells may have serious problems. You'd better tell me everything you know. Sit down."

Lorimer sat and recounted as much as he thought necessary. Forster listened in silence.

"So there's no real evidence O'Brien was murdered," he commented when Lorimer finished, "only rumours and suspicions."

"I'd say they are more than that."

"I dare say you would." Forster came upright. "But that's all they are. People out there are always imagining plots and intrigue, it's part of their way of life, and you don't seem to have done anything to stop the rumours. All right, you can go now, but I warn you, I shall be letting the Chairman know what I think about your conduct."

Lorimer, who had disobeyed Grantley's implied order by going to see Janet, would have preferred Forster to fob off Stephen with a half-apology that meant nothing, and let the matter die a natural death. But if the Managing Director was determined to make an issue of his going, he couldn't stop him. Forster was ambitious. His bonhomie was a pose, strip it away and he was rough, hard and self-seeking. Lorimer suspected that he didn't really care anything for Janet O'Brien's feelings; his pride was piqued because the Chairman had said who was to go out to Shajiha, and he was taking his pique out on him. Hurt the vanity of a powerful man and it was surprising how petty and malicious he might well be.

Maybe he should have told Forster about his being shot at and his flat being watched, Lorimer thought. He might have conceded then that there was more to Hassan's theory than mere gossip and imaginings. There hadn't seemed any point in doing so.

On his way out he asked Forster's secretary where he could find Maxwells' personnel department.

"It's on the left at the end of this corridor," Sandra Francis told him.

The pub had seen better days. Its stucco was worn and peeling like dead skin from an old wound, and even the brewer's name over the row of three tall sash windows was fading. In the saloon bar, half dark at six o'clock on that fine summer evening, the mahogany and brass looked dingy. The Golden Lion was a relic of another age, when the harbour had been busy day in and day out, before the switch to container traffic had seen most of its trade move to other, more modern ports. An air of depression and neglect hung over it, just as it did over the whole town. At the long quays, where the idle cranes stood like beckoning skeletons, a single cargo vessel was tied up.

Even the beer was flat, Lorimer thought. As if the atmosphere had affected it too. Perhaps the landlord no longer cared.

"You say you're from head office?" the young man with him asked. His name was Lyddon and he looked about twenty, although he must have been older than that, stocky, with gingerish hair and strangely innocent blue eyes. He drank a third of his pint with relish; it was the first real beer he had tasted for weeks, and he hardly noticed that it was flat.

Lorimer nodded. "That's right," he agreed. He had had his own reasons for picking the *Maxwell Pride*'s third officer to talk to. For one thing, if only two or three people on the ship were involved in O'Brien's racket, Lyddon was unlikely to be one of them. He hadn't enough authority. For another, a young man with his career to make might be less inclined to ask awkward questions. And third, an officer, even a very junior one, would be in a better position to give him the information he wanted than one of the crew.

"We only docked this afternoon," Lyddon said in a tone that was half wondering, half resentful. He wanted to start on his way to his home in the Midlands.

"I know," Lorimer said. "This won't take long." He didn't add that

that, too, was something he had learned in Maxwells' personnel department that morning, nor that he had waited for nearly three hours for the *Maxwell Pride* to dock and Lyddon to come ashore, watching the ship inch her way into the quay. She was an unlovely vessel, designed for utility rather than appearance.

"What do you want to know?" Lyddon asked.

"Nothing much. Have you ever taken on any passengers at Dhartoum?"

Lorimer knew it was possible that Lyddon would lie, the *Maxwell Pride* wasn't supposed to carry passengers, but he believed he was telling the truth when he answered, "Passengers? We haven't had any since I joined her."

His surprise appeared to be genuine, and Lorimer's hopes sank a little. "Any stowaways?" he inquired.

"No."

How had O'Brien got the prisoners aboard then? Suddenly Lorimer remembered something Oldfield had mentioned casually. "You've taken on extra hands there sometimes, haven't you?" he asked.

"Those clowns!" Lyddon sounded disgusted. "We were supposed to take one this voyage, but he didn't show up. Got another job, I suppose. We didn't want him anyway. They're a funny lot in the office out there, they're always arranging extra crew when we don't want anybody. Jock Hastings said something about it to the skipper once, but the Old Man told him that if the office wanted us to have them, there wasn't much we could do about it. They're bloody useless, they either go sick or they jump ship."

"Where do they jump ship?" Lorimer asked curiously.

"Piraeus, two of them. And one at Genoa. A couple of voyages back we had one went sick in Bilbao, and we had to leave him there. Jock thought he was putting it on, but the Captain said forget it, we'd had enough of him and it was good riddance. Too damn right!" Lyddon added with feeling.

Lorimer suspected he had had most to do with the men. "Were they Arabs?" he asked, hoping he had achieved the right note of casual interest.

"The two who scarpered at Piraeus were. The one we left at Bilbao was a Spaniard. Another time there was an Italian; he was the one legged it in Genoa." Lyddon finished his beer. "Bloody useless they were."

Lorimer wasn't surprised. "How long have you been on the *Maxwell Pride?*" he asked.

"About three years."

"Do you like it?"

"The job, you mean? Sure, it's great." Lyddon eyed his empty glass and wondered whether he should offer to buy this man from head office a drink. Who was he, anyway?

Lorimer saw his glance. "Another pint?" he suggested. He believed he knew now how O'Brien had smuggled the prisoners out of Shajiha. Most of them were probably professional men or political activists, it was hardly to be wondered at if they made poor hands.

At ten forty-five Southwold Terrace was deserted. Lorimer had looked in at the pub round the corner, but there was nobody there he knew, and after one quick drink he left. He had nearly reached number 15 when a movement in the shadows across the street reminded him of the man he had seen watching the flat. He ran across, but there was no sign of anyone. Either he had been mistaken, or whoever it was had gone into the block of flats. He could hardly follow them there to tackle them. Frustrated and annoyed, Lorimer crossed back to the other side.

His flat was on the second floor. On the first landing a light showed under the door opposite the stairs, while from behind it came a roar of rock music. Feeling in his pocket for his key, Lorimer started up the second flight.

As soon as he opened the door, he knew somebody had been in his flat. They had made no attempt to conceal it—the small table in the hall was lying on its side, and when he entered the living room it was a shambles. Furniture had been pushed about or overturned, pictures torn from the walls and drawers pulled out, their contents strewn over the floor.

His first reaction was fury, replaced almost immediately by anger mixed with curiosity. This wasn't the work of a professional housebreaker; professionals worked methodically and whoever had been here had set about the job with about as much method as a bull in a china shop. He heard something and stopped, one hand on the back of a chair he had been about to stand on its feet. The sound, slight though it was, was unmistakable: a stifled cough. And it came from his bedroom.

Lorimer strode across the living room and thrust open the door. The bedroom was in darkness, but by the light behind him he could see the wardrobe, one of its doors open, and the foot of the bed. He pushed the door wider, reaching out his right hand for the light switch. As he did so, the door was slammed hard against him and something hit his left shoulder a crushing blow. Caught off balance, he half-fell against the wall.

"You okay, Bill?" a man whispered urgently somewhere behind the door.

Another man grunted assent.

Arms wrapped themselves round Lorimer from behind and he was half-thrown, half-bundled to the floor. His head crashed into the skirting board with sickening force. Through a haze he felt two men push past him and heard the flat door slam.

For several seconds he remained there, stunned. Then, shaking his head, he hauled himself groggily to his feet. He wasn't hurt, except for a badly bruised shoulder, but he was angry, partly with the two men, but more with himself. He had behaved like a prize fool charging in like that. He should have barricaded the bedroom door with the sideboard or an easy chair or something, that would have kept them in the bedroom long enough for him to telephone the police. Instead, he had rushed in like a moron, they had escaped, and he knew nothing about them or why they had been here.

The first thing was to see what, if anything, was missing, then he would call the police. There was no point in doing that if they had taken nothing.

The bedroom had hardly been disturbed, but it took Lorimer some time to restore something like order to the living room. By the time he had finished he was satisfied nothing had been taken. He didn't possess much of value, but several small, easily portable and disposable things like a pair of silver tankards and his father's dress studs were in their usual places. On the other hand, the drawer in which he kept personal papers, and the filing box containing receipts and so on had been ransacked. The men weren't ordinary thieves; it was clear they had been looking for something, and very likely the chaos they had caused was intended to mislead him and the police.

The police. There was nothing to be gained by calling them; nothing had been stolen. Lorimer walked to the window and looked out. A man was back there across the street, watching this house. There must be two or three of them, taking it in turns. Was it one of them who had followed him in the red Sierra yesterday? If so, they had probably followed him to his meeting with Lyddon today also.

Lorimer wondered if the one over there now had been acting as a look-out for the intruders. If so, the fact that he was still there might mean they had failed to find what they wanted and would return for it when he was out of the way. What was it?

Lorimer had no idea. But it seemed a safe bet that if there was anything, it was in some way connected with his trip to Shajiha. Letting the curtain fall back into place, he picked up his phone and dialled Rosalind's number.

There was a lengthy wait, and he had concluded she was in bed and probably asleep when she said, "Hallo?"

"It's Gray," he told her.

"Oh!" Rosalind said angrily. Somewhere, very faintly, a man murmured something. "What on earth are you ringing for at this time of night?"

Unreasonably, Lorimer felt she was failing him. "Something's happened," he told her. "Will you have lunch with me tomorrow?"

"No, I won't," Rosalind said more angrily than before. "Can't you understand, Gray, I have my own life now? You're not part of it any more."

"All right, forget it," Lorimer said.

He put the phone down. She was right, of course, and it was illogical to feel this gnawing resentment. It was what they had both wanted. Or, at least, what they had mutually decided was best.

She had had people with her. No, specifically, she had had a man. Well, she had every right to, it was no longer any business of his. It didn't stop his feeling angry and let down.

Going out to the kitchen, he made himself some coffee. As he was pouring the water into the pot the phone rang. Who the hell was calling him now? he wondered, putting the kettle down and going to answer it.

"Gray?" It was Rosalind. "I'm sorry about just now. Do you still want to see me tomorrow?"

"It's all right," Lorimer said.

"I can't manage lunch, I've got to feed a client. Would coffee be all right?"

"You've got somebody there." He was careful to keep any note of accusation out of his voice, to make it a simple statement of fact, giving her a reason for hanging up if she wanted to.

"He's gone; he only came in for a drink after the concert. He was leaving when you rang. We'd been to the Festival Hall."

"What was it?" Lorimer asked.

"The LSO. Brahms and Haydn."

Rosalind had always loved music, and in the old days they had gone to concerts together fairly regularly. It was months since Lorimer had been to one now.

"Coffee would be fine," he said.

"What's going on?" Rosalind demanded.

"I don't know," Lorimer confessed. "I'd been to the pub. When I got back the flat was a shambles, furniture knocked over, drawers emptied on the floor, the lot. Then I heard somebody in the bedroom. There were two of them. They knocked me down, bundled me out of the way, and scarpered."

"Are you all right?"

"Apart from a sore head. I banged it on the skirting."

"It's hard enough, you'll survive," Rosalind commented unsympathetically. "They didn't damage our table, did they?" She and Lorimer had bought a small sofa table at a country sale soon after they were married. When they split up she had insisted, with real generosity, for she was very fond of it, that Lorimer kept it, because he had agreed to her having several things they both liked.

He shook his head. "That's all right."

"Oh, good. Did they take much?"

"Nothing. They weren't ordinary thieves, they were looking for something."

"Are you serious?" Rosalind asked, frowning.

"Yes."

"What are you getting mixed up in, Gray? You said they're still watching your flat. Who are?"

"I don't know," Lorimer admitted. "There's been a man outside for the last two days."

"Have you told the police about him? And the break-in?"

"No. It would only mean a lot of questions, and nothing's been taken."

Rosalind looked concerned. "The last I heard, you were flying out to Shajiha because somebody who worked for United had committed suicide out there," she said.

"I went." Lorimer paused. He found it embarrassing asking her, but he wanted confirmation and he couldn't think of anybody else to ask. "Can you imagine you still—well, care for me a bit?" he wanted to know. "Not very much."

Rosalind eyed him warily. "It'll take a lot of imagination, but I'll try."

"I'm serious."

"What makes you think I'm not?" She smiled sweetly. "All right, Gray, I'm sorry. But I'm not sure I'm prepared to commit myself even as far as that. You have a nasty sneaky way of taking advantage of things I say when I . . ."

"When you what?" Lorimer asked.

"It doesn't matter."

"All right. If you did, and I was supposed to have committed suicide but there was more than a chance I was really murdered, which would you want to believe?"

Rosalind stared at him. "They're not very pleasant alternatives. I'd rather think you'd been murdered, I suppose; I'd hate to believe you'd got to such a pitch you'd killed yourself. Anybody would, I should think."

"That's what I thought," Lorimer agreed. "But Janet O'Brien's adamant that her husband committed suicide. She's even told their children he did."

"And there's a possibility he didn't?"

"More than a possibility. I know he didn't."

"Does that mean you think she killed him?"

"No, that was some people out there. He'd got himself mixed up in a dangerous business."

Rosalind put down her coffee-cup and regarded her ex-husband gravely. "And now you are too, aren't you?" she said. "I thought it was going to be an ordinary, rather sad, routine trip."

"So did I."

"And it wasn't."

"No." Lorimer wondered whether O'Brien had understood all along just how dangerous a game he was playing, or if he had only realized it when it was too late.

"I'm glad I didn't know," Rosalind told him. "I'd have been worried sick." She saw his surprise and added impatiently, "Don't be silly, Gray. And you needn't look so bloody pleased with yourself, I'd have felt the same whoever it was."

Lorimer noticed the touch of colour that had come to her cheeks but he said nothing.

"Do you want some more coffee?" Rosalind asked after a moment, her tone challenging.

"No, thanks."

There was a brief silence before she said, "Why do you have to involve yourself in whatever it is? Why not leave it to other people? It's their job."

"That's what Grantley said," Lorimer remarked. "He told me to bury it."

"Well, why don't you? If that man O'Brien really was murdered, it's up to the Shajihan police. You can't do anything."

Nor would they, now Hassan was dead, Lorimer reflected.

"I just don't like it," he said. "I don't like people I know being murdered, and I don't like being shot at. Or watched all the time." Maybe it wasn't a very adequate reason for mixing himself up in whatever was going on, but wasn't it the truth? He had become involved through no fault of his own, and he had no intention of sitting back and waiting for whatever the men who killed O'Brien planned for him.

But there was more to it than that, and he wasn't yet ready to tell anybody all of it. Not even Rosalind. He saw she was gazing at him, her lovely forehead creased in a frown and her eyes concerned, and remembered he hadn't meant to tell her about the shots fired at his taxi.

"When were you shot at?" she demanded.

"In the taxi on the way from the airport."

For a moment Rosalind didn't speak, then she said quietly, "Take care of yourself, Gray."

"I mean to," Lorimer assured her.

"I don't want to hear you've been killed too. I look ghastly in black."

It was a lie, he thought. She looked stunning in black.

TEN

Immaculate lawns reached as far as the river bank where girls in summer dresses were stretched out on the grass eating sandwiches. Nearer at hand the flower-beds were a mass of scarlet, yellow and blue blossoms, while behind the two men as they walked, and a little way off, the pinnacled silhouette of King's College Chapel stood out against the clear blue sky. Lorimer looked round appreciatively.

"I'm afraid one does tend to take it all rather for granted," Humphrey Downing remarked apologetically.

"I'm sorry?" Lorimer said.

"All this. After a while. I remember when I first came up I found it all a little overwhelming. We had more sense of reverence in those days. Too much, perhaps." Downing was nearly seventy, a tall, spare figure, despite a lifetime of good living. He rather resembled a dry, slightly bent stick, its bark rubbed away in places to reveal the grey wood underneath, Lorimer thought. "There was an American here once. A tourist. He asked our head gardener how he achieved such perfect lawns. 'We cut 'em and roll 'em, sir. Just cut and roll,' old Manley told him. 'I cut and roll mine back home, but I can't get anything like these,' the American protested. Old Manley looked at him with a face as straight as that path. 'Ah, but then we've been doing it for five hundred years, sir,' he said." Downing chuckled quietly. "There's something very reassuring about such continuity. You won't appreciate it now, but when you're my age, reassurance counts for a good deal."

Lorimer thought of his own university's brand-new campus. This was beautiful, but what right had men like Downing to be complacent or assume superiority merely because of their inheritance? Most of it was paid for by poor sods of wage-earners who never even saw it, let alone enjoyed its privileges. All the same, there was something, and perhaps Downing wasn't complacent, only proud in an embarrassed, English way.

"You said on the phone you wanted to have a word with me about one of my old students," the old man reminded him, walking on along the gravel path that led to the college bridge.

"Ahmad Hassan," Lorimer said.

"Hassan? Why come to me?"

"His wife said you knew him better than anyone in England. And that he'd kept in touch with you. You know he's dead?"

Downing stopped and looked at his companion. "No. When did it happen?"

Despite his denial, Lorimer was pretty sure the old man had already known about Hassan's death. So why had he denied it?

"Last Friday," he answered. "Somebody planted a bomb under his car."

Downing walked on. "I'm sorry. Very sorry. I take it you knew him then?"

"Slightly. I had dinner with him and his wife the evening before he was killed." Not for the first time Lorimer found it difficult to say how well he had known Hassan; it still seemed much better than a mere couple of days' acquaintance implied.

"Do they know who did it?" Downing asked.

"I don't know; I came home on Sunday." Lorimer paused. "Do you know what he was doing?"

The old man gave him a sideways look that said nothing. "He left Cambridge fourteen or fifteen years ago. I've hardly seen him since then."

"His wife said he was an Inspector in the Security Police."

"Was he?"

"I hoped you would tell me something about him."

"Did you? Why are you interested in him?"

Lorimer hesitated. Downing's habit of talking almost exclusively in questions created difficulties, and he suspected that if he gave the wrong answer, the old man would tell him nothing. But what answer was the right one? "A colleague of mine was killed out there," he said. "They sent me out to help his widow and deal with the formalities. Ahmad Hassan was interested in the way he died."

"Really? And you say he was in the Security Police. What was your colleague's job, Mr. Lorimer? But perhaps I shouldn't ask."

"Why not?" Lorimer said. "He was the Overseas Manager of a transport company. He was out there on a routine visit to the local office in Dhartoum. Hassan was only interested in his death indirectly."

"Oh, I see." Humphrey Downing smiled. But the smile didn't touch his eyes; only his thin, pale lips moved slightly. His tone fastidiously polite, he said, "Forgive my curiosity."

"From what Hassan said, I gathered something was going on in Shajiha," Lorimer told him.

"Isn't something always going on everywhere, even in Shajiha? Perhaps especially in Shajiha?" This time the half-smile was warmer. "I'm afraid I know very little about Middle Eastern affairs, but I can't see any harm in my telling you what little I can about Hassan. You know his father edited a newspaper and came to this country because he fell foul of the old regime? Ahmad was a brilliant student. Quite exceptional. And a charming young man, too. He was doing some very good work here, then there was the revolution in Shajiha, the monarchy was overthrown, and he went back. I always thought he rather regretted leaving Cambridge, but he felt he had to go. We corresponded occasionally, but as I say, I've only seen him once or twice since he went."

"What sort of man was he?" Lorimer asked. "Apart from his brilliance and charm?"

"Sort of man?" Downing looked slightly irritated. "I do dislike the modern desire to categorize people. It's a form of laziness. How can you say anyone was a group A or whatever?"

"Well, would you say he was an idealist?" Lorimer suggested.

The old man considered the question. "Yes, I think perhaps that might be a fair comment," he conceded. "Though he was by no means a blind one. I always found him a rather complex character, intelligent, charming, generous, energetic—and, possibly, quite ruthless."

"Ruthless?" Lorimer repeated, surprised. "Why do you say that?" Why should he be surprised? he wondered. After all, hadn't he thought much the same? It was only Downing's thinking so, and being prepared to admit it, he found surprising.

"It was merely a feeling I got."

"Do you think he would be loyal to what he believed in?"

"Oh, I would imagine so. Yes, quite definitely. And almost incorruptible."

"Almost?"

"All men are corruptible," Downing said. "By dreams, ideals, power."

They walked on, over the humpbacked bridge beyond which the college grounds extended another couple of hundred yards or so to Queen's Road. Under the bridge a young woman in a T-shirt and shorts was inexpertly poling a punt downstream, watched anxiously by a young man reclining on cushions in the bows. There was an ominous thud, and after a delay of several seconds the punt emerged on the other side of the bridge heading towards the left-hand bank.

"For Chrissake, Jo!" the young man exclaimed in anguished tones.

"Get knotted," the girl told him succinctly.

Humphrey Downing smiled sadly.

"So you wouldn't describe Hassan as a liberal with a small *l?*" Lorimer suggested. For some time now he had wondered whether the Shajihan Inspector might have sympathized with, if not actually been involved in, O'Brien's venture. After all, it was possible O'Brien had acted from a misguided idealism.

"Why not? Who is more ruthless than your true liberal—with a small *l?*" Downing looked rather pleased with himself.

Damned old fool, Lorimer thought. But he knew it was untrue, and the old man was anything but a fool. He was watching him out of the corner of his eye now, his expression whimsically amused.

"Perhaps I went too far," he said. "As far as I know, he never did anything that suggested undue ruthlessness. I would say, if you pressed me, that he was above all a patriot. He looked at his own country with the romantic eyes of the exile; he wanted to make it a Utopia. Yet underneath it he was a realist. But that was when I knew him, a long time ago; experience changes us all."

"Doesn't a patriot usually remain one?" Lorimer asked.

"Ah, that depends on what you mean by patriotism." Downing looked gratified, as if his companion had walked into a carefully prepared semantic trap. "Loyalty to a blinkered view of one's own country, perhaps? Or to one's friends? But if you mean loyalty to a regime,

I imagine that can be much more easily destroyed. Revolutionaries, of course, invariably regard themselves as true patriots."

"And Hassan?" Lorimer inquired.

"Ah, I wonder." They were walking along a path sheltered on the left by a row of poplars towards a handsome wrought-iron gate that led to the road. "We may as well turn back here," Downing said. "All this is very interesting, but I'm afraid I can't see what it has to do with your colleague who was killed in Shajiha. Is there a connection?"

"I don't know," Lorimer admitted. He was groping in the dark, he thought, guided by nothing more tangible than a few things Hassan had said, and his own feelings. Even they were vague. "Would Hassan have actively opposed people in authority he believed were abusing their power?" he asked.

The old man considered. "He might have done. I'd go so far as to say he probably would. I'd like to think we instilled so much of our outlook and values into him while he was here."

You arrogant old bastard! Lorimer thought. Then he saw that his companion was smiling in a slightly vulpine way. "After all, that is your function, isn't it?" he agreed.

Downing looked disconcerted and slightly annoyed, and for a moment he said nothing. Then he observed casually, "I assume you had some actual situation in mind?"

"Maybe," Lorimer said. "Do you know anything about the prison camp at Al Faktum?"

This time the silence was more prolonged.

"I didn't know there was one," Downing answered.

You're lying, Lorimer told himself. They had almost reached the bridge again. Girls, their lunch-hour nearly over, were standing up and straightening their dresses, ready to walk back to their offices and shops. Mary Hassan had worked in a Cambridge bank; had she brought her lunch here to eat it by the river on warm summer days? Perhaps met Hassan here? The sound of the traffic in Trinity Street was no more than a muted rumble. Lorimer was hardly aware of it. Why should Downing lie about the camp? That he had done so must be significant. If only he could see how.

"You look thoughtful," Downing remarked.

"You've given me a lot to think about."

"Oh? Then let me tell you a little more. The Shajihan government is moderate and generally pro-West, but there are factions in the country which are neither, and they virtually control parts of it, just as the different sects do in Lebanon. They're fervently anti-West, especially anti-American. They want unrest throughout the whole Middle East, and over the last three or four years they've been actively involved in Lebanon and Israel. Anybody stirring up trouble in the region they'll support."

"The Hizbollah," Lorimer suggested.

Downing gave him a surprisingly sharp sideways look. "Yes," he agreed. "Exactly."

"So there are prison camps."

"Perhaps." Downing paused. "What has all this to do with Ahmad Hassan?"

"I'm not sure just now," Lorimer replied, "but it could have a lot."

They came to the wide arch that led under part of the college buildings to the big grassed court, and suddenly the air was much cooler.

"I'm afraid I haven't been able to help you much," Downing said with a return of his former deprecatory manner.

"You have," Lorimer assured him.

"Really?"

It occurred to the younger man there was something quizzical in Downing's expression, a suggestion of hidden amusement. He told himself he was probably mistaken. They shook hands, and he walked past the porter's lodge out by the great sixteenth-century gate into the street.

On the way back to his flat he stopped to pick up the film he had left to be processed. Two of the shots were blurred and indistinct, but in the others the face of the man watching the flat was sharp and clear.

The phone was ringing when he let himself in. It was Melissa.

"Would you like to take me out this evening?" she asked.

Lorimer wondered which of her boy-friends had let her down at the last minute, leaving her with a blank evening to fill. "Very much," he answered.

"Good. I hoped you would."

"Where do you want to go?"

"I don't care, just as long as the food's good and there's plenty of it. I'm *starving,* I hardly had any lunch."

"One of these days . . ." Lorimer began.

"I know, isn't it awful? Come about seven?"

"Will your father be there?"

Melissa lived with her father in a flat in Chelsea he had bought three years after her mother divorced him. It was small, convenient, and very expensive.

"No, he's got a business dinner this evening. Why?"

"He's out for my blood. I don't want it spilt over you."

"Is he?" Melissa giggled. "You don't want to bother about him. See you."

Lorimer put down the phone and looked at his watch. It was just after three. With any luck, Oldfield would still be at his office.

"You're sure you don't want to go on anywhere?" Lorimer asked.

Melissa shook her head. In the dim light of the restaurant her eyes looked even larger and brighter than usual. "Let's go to your place," she said.

In the taxi she snuggled up to him. "What is it, Gray?" she asked.

"What's what?"

"You have something on your mind; you have had all the evening. I like my men to give me their undivided attention."

"It's nothing," Lorimer told her. She was right, he thought. He had been thinking about O'Brien and Hassan and his conversation with Humphrey Downing, but he wasn't going to tell her about any of them. It wasn't that he didn't trust her, they just had nothing to do with her. Forget them and enjoy yourself.

Southwold Terrace was deserted save for an elderly man taking his dog for a walk. As Lorimer waited for the driver to give him his change, he glanced across the road. Nothing moved in the shadows by the entrance to the block of flats.

"Night, sir," the driver said.

"Night," Lorimer responded.

Melissa took his arm. In the room at the top of the first flight of stairs a noisy party was in progress. They climbed the second flight and stopped outside his door while he found his key.

"What would you do if you'd lost it?" Melissa wanted to know.

"Swear," Lorimer replied. He found the key and pushed it into the lock. "Tiny, in the next door flat, has a spare one, and I have one of his."

"I liked Tiny." Melissa had met him the other evening on her way out with Lorimer.

"Good." Lorimer opened the door. She walked into the living room, turned, and held out her arms. Her eyes were shining and her lips were slightly parted.

Melissa sighed rapturously. "My mother used to say one shouldn't take exercise on a full stomach," she remarked. "Do you think this is what she meant?" Turning, she half-propped herself up on one elbow. "Have you any strawberries?"

"No," Lorimer told her. "No strawberries."

"I feel like strawberries and cream," Melissa said regretfully.

At that moment the doorbell rang. Lorimer swore.

"Let it ring," Melissa said.

Lorimer hesitated. He was tempted to. Then there was a second ring, louder and more prolonged than the first.

"If the building's on fire, I don't care," Melissa murmured.

"I'd better go," Lorimer said. "If I don't, they'll just keep on."

Cursing inwardly, he pulled on his trousers and a dressing-gown, and padded across the living room.

There were two men on the landing. The older was about forty, not tall, but dark and wiry. He was wearing a lightweight casual jacket and dark trousers. His companion, who had his finger on the bell, was ten or twelve years younger, taller and flaxen-haired, in a leather jacket and jeans. There was about both of them an assurance, a suggestion of hardness that hinted at more than a passing acquaintance with violence.

"Mr. Graham Lorimer?" the older one asked. His voice, with a slight Welsh accent, hardly suggested the back streets.

"Yes," Lorimer agreed guardedly. "Who are you?"

His question was ignored. "We'd like a few words with you, Mr. Lorimer. Perhaps we might come in?"

"No." Lorimer didn't know who the two men were, nor did he much care, unless they were last night's intruders returned for whatever they hadn't found then; he had been messed about enough these last few days.

"It would be best if we did," the Welshman said reasonably. "We have every right to, but we'd rather have your consent." He produced a paper, unfolded it, and showed it to Lorimer.

Lorimer had never seen a search-warrant, but the document appeared to be one. "What's this all about?" he demanded. It was all a mistake, he told himself. It must be. Why should the police want to search his flat?

Without actually pushing him aside, the two men walked past him into the flat and the younger one closed the door.

"Perhaps we might deal with first things first," his companion suggested. He possessed an unmistakable air of authority. "Clive?"

The younger one started towards the bedroom door.

"Just a minute," Lorimer said angrily, making a move to intercept him. "Who the hell are you?" Neither of the men answered. "All right, why are you here?"

"Just to ask you a few questions," the older one replied. He glanced at the bedroom door. "If there's somebody in there, it would be less embarrassing for them if they came out."

The door opened and Melissa appeared there draped in the duvet, her hair dishevelled. She looked very beautiful and extremely cross.

"Who are you, miss?" the man called Clive asked her.

"That can't possibly be the slightest concern of yours."

"I'm afraid it is," the Welshman said.

Their eyes met.

"My name is Melissa Forster." Her voice sounded as if it would cut glass.

"You live here, Miss Forster?"

"I do not!"

Some men might have quailed at Melissa's tone, but the Welshman merely nodded impassively. "I beg your pardon," he apologized.

"I suppose you're some sort of private detective. I thought they always wore grubby raincoats."

"No," Lorimer said, "they're not private detectives." Private detectives, he thought, didn't come armed with search-warrants.

"So who are you? I want to know, because I have every intention of reporting you for barging in and behaving like this."

"Certainly. That's your right, Miss Forster. My name is Jenkins." He sounded mildly amused, which only made Melissa angrier.

"Do you think you're going to find drugs here?" she demanded scornfully.

"Are we?" Jenkins looked at Lorimer.

"No," Lorimer said.

"Actually, we're not specially interested in drugs. Only indirectly."

"So what are you interested in?"

Jenkins ignored Melissa's question. "Perhaps you would get dressed, then go with my colleague and give him your address," he said. "He'll call a taxi to take you home."

Melissa looked at Lorimer.

"Maybe it would be best," he told her.

"Hell! Aren't you going to *do* anything?"

"Perhaps. Later."

She stared at him for two or three seconds, then turned and went back into the bedroom, slamming the door behind her.

"You don't mind if we have a look round?" Jenkins asked.

Lorimer shrugged. "Does it make any difference?"

"Not really."

The two men set to work methodically.

After some minutes Melissa reappeared, still simmering with anger, but fully dressed and her make-up repaired. Without glancing at any of the three men she crossed the room and went out, calling, "Good night, Gray," over her shoulder in a contemptuous, resentful tone. The younger man, Clive, followed her.

"Have you finished looking for whatever it is?" Lorimer demanded bitterly.

"We didn't expect to find anything, but we had to look, just in case," Jenkins told him. "Shall we sit down?"

"Why? You aren't staying."

"I hope you're right. I've been on duty since eight this morning, and I've hardly seen my family for a week."

"You come bursting in here with a search-warrant. . . ." Lorimer's anger was fading, and he was more curious than resentful. "All right," he agreed, sitting on the end of the sofa.

Jenkins took an easy chair facing him. "I'm sorry if we came at an inconvenient time," he apologized gravely.

"You did. Why did you have to come at nearly midnight?"

"It might have been rather urgent."

"What might?" Lorimer thought he knew who Jenkins was—or, rather, whom he worked for. Partly it was his manner, his air of quiet assurance that spoke of officialdom. But why should M.I.5 or the Special Branch be interested in him?

The Welshman didn't reply immediately, and when he did it was with another question. "What is your interest in Shajiha?" he asked.

"Minimal," Lorimer answered.

"You spent several days there last week."

"Because my firm sent me out. One of their managers died there and they wanted somebody to sort out the local red tape and see his widow was all right."

"Michael O'Brien, Overseas Manager of Maxwells."

There was no point in asking Jenkins how he knew. In any case, *how* interested Lorimer less than *how much*. "Did your other two not find what they wanted?" he inquired.

Jenkins looked puzzled. "Other two?"

"The men who were here when I came home last night. They were searching the place."

"What were they like?"

"I don't know. It was dark, I didn't see their faces—and they weren't as polite as you, they didn't introduce themselves. They were in the bedroom. When I went in there, they knocked me down and cleared off."

"What made you think I might know them?" Jenkins asked.

"They were English, Londoners very likely. One of them called the other Bill."

"They weren't ours."

"Who are yours?" Jenkins smiled faintly. "All right. They'd turned the place upside-down while I was out, but they didn't take anything. Why is everybody so interested in me all of a sudden?"

"Somebody else is?"

"There's been a man watching this flat for most of the last two days."

"We've no reason to watch you, Mr. Lorimer. All I've come for now is a little chat to clear up one or two questions, nothing more."

"Then who is he? And whose car followed me back from Surrey the day before yesterday?"

"I've no idea. What's this man like?"

"About thirty, medium height, thin. He looks like an Arab." Lorimer stood up. "I've got some pictures of him."

He went into the bedroom, found the paper wallet of prints, and returned to the living room. "That's him," he said, handing Jenkins the two clear photographs. "Do you know him?"

Jenkins studied the pictures with interest, and nodded. "His name's Muhammad Ghanim. He's a chauffeur at the Shajihan embassy."

"*A what?*" Lorimer asked.

Jenkins smiled. "It isn't only in the Russian delegations people aren't always what they pretend to be. Your friend is a member of the Shajihan intelligence service."

Lorimer stared at him. "O'Brien and Hassan are killed out there and I'm shot at. When I get home I'm followed and watched. My flat's broken into. Then you come. What the hell's going on?"

"I hoped you would tell me," the Welshman said gravely.

"All I know is that O'Brien was murdered and it was made to look as if he'd committed suicide, and that he was smuggling prisoners from the camp at Al Faktum out of the country."

"Prisoners?"

"It's a prison camp."

"There's only one camp at Al Faktum," Jenkins said. "And it's not a prison, it's the world's most important base for training terrorists."

ELEVEN

Lorimer was stunned.

"Extremist groups all over the world send their top operational men there," Jenkins went on. "The IRA, ETA, the Red Brigades, the Japanese Red Army, some of the most extreme Palestinian factions—you name it, they go there. A lot of East European arms find their way to Al Faktum and out again, too."

Lorimer remembered Mary Hassan's telling him on the phone that her husband had trusted him. Perhaps it was true up to a point, he would like to think so, but Hassan hadn't trusted him enough to tell him the truth about the camp. Maybe experience had taught him to be cautious, and at the last moment, when he was on the point of revealing what he knew, he had drawn back, not quite sure enough. Or was it that he, a genuine patriot, had balked at admitting to a virtual stranger that people in his country trained and armed terrorists to spread carnage and misery through half the civilized world?

As for O'Brien, if he hadn't been playing the Scarlet Pimpernel, what was he doing? Was Hassan's first suggestion right, and he had been spying on the camp, perhaps for British Intelligence?

That was possible, but it didn't explain the second man who, Hassan believed, had come from the camp, and whom O'Brien had apparently been there to meet. Was he the real spy, and O'Brien's job had been merely to pick him up and ship him out of the country? Lorimer would have been more inclined to believe so if it hadn't been for the men O'Brien had arranged the *Maxwell Pride* should take on as additional crew. According to Lyddon, at least two of them were Arabs, one a Spaniard and another an Italian. Were the first two Palestinian terrorists, and the others members of ETA and the Red Brigades? The man whose body had been washed up the day after O'Brien's "suicide" was carrying a passport in the name of Sullivan;

that was as Irish as O'Brien, and Hassan thought it was Sullivan Maxwells' Overseas Manager had picked up near the camp.

The glaring probability was that O'Brien had been smuggling not political refugees but terrorists out of Shajiha, and when they reached their destinations they either reported sick and had to be left behind, or they jumped ship. Janet had said his job was getting on top of him. Perhaps the truth was that he had lost his nerve and been killed because, no longer reliable, he was becoming a threat to the safety of the men who employed him. If so, and Janet knew, it was no wonder she was scared.

Everyone seemed to be conspiring to put up a smoke-screen to conceal what was really going on, Lorimer thought. No, a sandscreen, denser, more impenetrable than any smoke-screen. "Who runs the camp?" he asked.

"One of the extremist groups," Jenkins replied.

According to Downing, extremists of one sort or another more or less controlled parts of Shajiha. If they were behind the camp, Hassan might well have fallen foul of them, he wouldn't have wanted any truck with terrorism and subversion. But what had brought Jenkins and his colleague here tonight? Only one person knew about his interest in Hassan and Al Faktum.

"Humphrey Downing," Lorimer said flatly. "He put you on to me, didn't he?"

"Why did you go to see him?" Jenkins asked.

"I liked Hassan, I had dinner with him and his wife the night before he was killed. Mary Hassan said Downing was his tutor at Cambridge, and he knew him better than anyone else in Britain. They'd kept in touch since Hassan went back to Shajiha. Hassan was interested in what O'Brien was doing, and so was I."

"We all are."

"Do you know?"

Jenkins hesitated. "Not exactly. We know that terrorists are being trained at Al Faktum and turning up at trouble spots all over the world without passing through any passport controls. There's no secret about that."

"And you suspected O'Brien had a hand in it?"

"Not specifically him. Not even Maxwells. Then . . ." Jenkins paused. "Have you heard of a man named Sullivan whose body was washed up near Dhartoum a week ago?"

"Yes, Hassan mentioned him."

"The day after he was found the IRA put out one of their usual bulletins saying that an officer of theirs had been killed 'on active service.' His name was Sullivan, too." Jenkins stopped. "You don't seem surprised."

"I'm not," Lorimer said. "What happens now?"

"I don't suppose we shall have to trouble you again, but if you take my advice, you'll keep out of this business. Right out."

"I'm not in it," Lorimer retorted. "I'm fed up with telling people —United sent me out to check on things at the Dhartoum office, finish off any work O'Brien had been doing and help Mrs. O'Brien. The first I knew of any of the rest of it was when they tried to shoot me."

"In the taxi."

"You know about that?"

"Yes. They haven't tried anything since then, have they?"

"No." That was surprising, Lorimer thought. After all, he knew a lot more now than he had done then and he had asked a lot of questions. It looked as if "they," whoever "they" were, no longer regarded him as dangerous now that he had left Shajiha and they knew he wasn't taking over O'Brien's job.

When Jenkins had gone he poured himself a stiff Scotch. He toyed with the idea of ringing Melissa, but decided she was probably in bed by now and, in any case, it was unlikely she would exactly welcome a call from him. Also there was the possibility that her father would answer the phone, and Lorimer didn't want to talk to Forster.

Taking his glass out to the kitchen, he washed it and went to bed himself.

"Who were you out with last night?" Forster inquired, spreading marmalade on a slice of toast.

"Why?" Melissa wanted to know.

She was in one of her moods this morning, her father thought. Close as they were, there were times when he could cheerfully have hit her; she could be more difficult and infuriating than her mother had ever been.

He and Brenda had been divorced when it was clear she would be a liability to him in his climb up the ladder, both at Maxwells and socially. She had never made the slightest attempt to acquire even a veneer of polish; she was still the easygoing, slightly common woman he had married, and she had no intention of changing.

The divorce had hurt her, but that wasn't his fault. Even then she hadn't understood that she chained him to a past he was determined to put right behind him and, as far as possible, forget. Every time he looked at her in her drab clothes, her hair a mess, he felt he was being dragged down.

He had no idea what she was doing now. He supposed his solicitors would have told him if she had married again, but the bank paid over her allowance every month, and as far as he was concerned, that was the end of it. He didn't even know where she lived.

As he ate his toast he looked round the room with the feeling of satisfaction seeing his possessions always gave him. Forster's parents hadn't been really poor, but when he was a boy there had been very little money for luxuries, while the post-war austerity had lasted almost until he was in his teens. The films he had seen in his weekly visit to the cinema and the pre-war novels his mother encouraged him to read had filled him with dreams of a life where a degree of luxury was taken for granted.

Now he belonged to that world. He was a somebody instead of a nobody, and his achievement was symbolized in this flat. Here the tokens of his success were all round him; the expensive, slightly vulgar funiture, the bar in one corner of this room, the thick carpets and the pictures on the walls bought at Harrods in a single extravagant half-hour.

Dreams, Forster thought, were worth nothing if you didn't make them come true. It was possessions that mattered, and having the money to acquire them. Materialism brought progress, not idealism.

He looked across the table at his daughter. "It was Graham Lorimer, wasn't it?"

"Why ask me if you know?" Melissa had gone to bed angry and slept badly. This morning she had a headache, and she was ready to pick a quarrel with anybody. It was her father's misfortune he happened to be the only person around.

"Do you like him?" Forster asked.

"At the moment I detest him."

"What happened?" Melissa's expression told Forster nothing. She didn't answer, and he went on, "He has too good an opinion of himself. If he doesn't look out, he'll end up in serious trouble."

"That doesn't surprise me in the least." Melissa poured herself a second cup of coffee. It was black and strong, but it didn't seem to be doing her much good, and she had a meeting with Heathcotes this morning, which was sure to be difficult. "The police were at his flat last night," she said.

"Oh? Were you there?"

"For a very short time."

"What did they want?"

"Drugs, I suppose. They said they didn't, but you can't believe anything they say."

"Does Lorimer take drugs?" Forster frowned and helped himself to another slice of toast. To give Lorimer his due, he wouldn't have thought so.

"I haven't the slightest idea," Melissa replied with chilly detachment.

"Have you seen him often?"

"For God's sake! Why this inquisition? Two or three times. I don't know, I haven't counted. Last night we went out for a meal at some Italian restaurant, then back to his flat for a drink. The police came while I was there, two of them in plain clothes with a search-warrant. They were bloody rude. I said I'd report them."

"I shouldn't," Forster said.

"Why not?"

"It never does any good antagonizing the police, and I expect they were only doing their job. If they had a search-warrant, they must know something about Lorimer."

There was a brief silence before Melissa asked, "How did you know I was out with him last night?"

"Somebody I know saw you," her father replied. "Will you be in this evening?"

"I don't know." Gray had been right, Melissa thought, Dad really had it in for him.

There were a good many more people at the church than Lorimer had expected to see there. O'Brien must have been well liked, he thought. Forster had come with another man Lorimer remembered seeing in Maxwells' offices and O'Brien's secretary, a plump youngish woman who looked to be on the verge of tears.

There was a fairly large group of family mourners. Even allowing for their mourning, their clothes contrasted noticeably with those of the smart local people in the congregation, and Lorimer remembered Janet's telling him in Dhartoum that she and her husband didn't have any money of their own.

Stephen was sitting beside her at the end of a pew, with Juliet on her other side. Once before the service started he looked round, and as their glances met, Lorimer saw the hostility in the boy's eyes before he turned away.

The service ran its course, the hearse and the family cars departed for the crematorium three miles away, and the rest of the congregation filed out into the warm sunshine looking uncertain and slightly lost. Lorimer had no wish to come face-to-face with Forster, and he lingered so that he was almost the last to leave the church. When finally he did so, Forster and his two companions were already climbing into the Managing Director's BMW. He watched it drive off towards the main road, slid behind the wheel of his Saab, and followed.

He took his time driving back to London, and as far as he could see, he wasn't followed.

It was nearly seven when he arrived home that evening. As soon as he opened his door and stepped into the little hall, he smelt a familiar subtle fragrance. Melissa was reclining gracefully on the sofa in his living room wearing a grey-and-white dress with loose, filmy sleeves and a full skirt. Her right arm was draped along the sofa's back, and her left hanging down so that her beautifully shaped and painted nails nearly touched the carpet. Her skirt was pulled up a little at one side and her hair swung, a sleek dark curtain, across one side of her face. Lorimer wondered how long she had been waiting like that. He was pleased and surprised to see her.

"Hallo, Gray," she said softly.

"Hallo. How did you get in?"

"I borrowed your spare key from Tiny. He's awfully sweet, isn't he?" Melissa smiled a shade complacently.

"Awfully."

"I've been waiting ages. Aren't you glad to see me?"

"Very." Lorimer walked across to the window and looked out. There was nobody in the street obviously watching the flat; perhaps they were taking more care not to be spotted now.

"You don't seem glad," Melissa said, her lovely lips pouting. She stood up, went to join him, and kissed him with enthusiasm. "I was mad with you last night," she said. "You let that foul man ruin everything."

"There wasn't much I could do," Lorimer pointed out.

"What did he really want? Was it drugs?"

"No. He seemed to think I knew something about some people in Shajiha."

"But you were only there two or three days."

"Yes."

"Did you?"

"No. He didn't stay long."

"He got rid of me very effectively." Melissa fiddled with one of the buttons on Lorimer's jacket. "Dad knows about us."

Lorimer was surprised to find he didn't care very much. To hell with Forster, what could he do? "You told him?" he asked.

"No, of course I didn't. It's no business of his who I go out with. He told me at breakfast this morning; somebody saw us last night at that restaurant. I think he was warning me about you." Almost angrily, Melissa demanded, "For God's sake! You aren't afraid of him, are you?"

"No," Lorimer said. As if drawn by a magnet, he turned back to the window. He could still see nobody there.

"Why do you keep looking out at the street?" Melissa demanded.

He felt like telling her it was because an Arab intelligence man had been watching his flat, that somebody had tried to kill him in Shajiha, that O'Brien and another man had been murdered there, and that two days ago he had come home and found two men searching this flat. But what was the point? Apart from any other considerations, she wouldn't believe him.

"Habit," he said. "It must be living on my own."

"You'd better do something about that then." Melissa laughed. "Oh, I nearly forgot, there was a phone call for you. I thought I'd better answer it in case it was something important."

"Who was it?" Lorimer asked.

"Some woman. She said her name was Rosalind. I asked if I could give you a message, but she said, 'No, thank you,' and hung up. Who is she, Gray?"

"My wife," Lorimer said. Oh hell! he thought.

"What are you thinking about?"

Shajar Ali turned her head to look at the young man beside her. "Many things," she answered.

The warm breeze caressed her skin and stirred her hair. They were sitting on a slope between the perimeter fence of the camp and the end of one of the rows of concrete huts. The sun had set, and soon it would be lights out; early to bed was the rule at Al Faktum.

"Do you ever feel afraid, Shajar?" Ihsan asked in a tone that suggested that, if she did, he could understand her fear. Even, perhaps, that sometimes he shared it.

"What of?" the girl asked. "Dying? No, I'm not afraid." She was not afraid of dying, because any good Muslim who died fighting in a jihad was ensured of a place in heaven, but she did fear, in her darkest moments, pain and humiliation. Sometimes at night she woke in the dark, bleak dormitory, and her fear was so real that she lay there, dreading the coming of another day. When the day came, and she was fully occupied again, training, her fears dissolved, and she couldn't explain them to Ihsan now because one must not admit to fear. Especially if one was a woman.

Shajar was slight, with an oval, olive-skinned face and dark, serious eyes. In her drab-green uniform, her dark hair cut short, she looked both trim and efficient. She was a soldier, her whole being devoted absolutely to her cause, and she found it hard to remember now the months when she had been training to be a teacher, a girl from a poor village given a rare opportunity to attend the university. During her second year there, her father had been killed by the Israelis in Lebanon and it was soon after that she joined Hizbollah's army. Five months ago she had been singled out for special training and sent here to Al Faktum.

"I am afraid sometimes," Ihsan confessed.

"You?" Shajar was surprised, he always seemed so cool and confident.

"I start wondering what it will be like when we go into action and how I will behave. I wish I could be like others and look forward to the fighting, but I can't. I'm a planner, not a soldier."

Shajar was shocked. She had never heard anyone in the army talk in this way, and it seemed akin to treachery. She wished Ihsan hadn't told her.

For a little while, busy with their own thoughts, neither spoke, then she said, "I would like to marry sometime and have children, but that's impossible now. We have to fight, Ihsan."

"And die, if that is God's will," the boy agreed. He was only a little older than Shajar. "I heard two of the Irishmen talking this afternoon. They didn't know I speak English, or they didn't care. They said the one who left the other day was killed when he was on his way to lead an operation somewhere. Now his people will have to find someone to take his place." Ihsan paused. "I didn't like him, he was too hard, too callous."

"We have to be hard," Shajar said.

"I know, but . . . How would you feel if you were ordered to throw a bomb into a bus, or fire into a crowd at an airport, knowing little children would be killed?"

"One mustn't think of them as people. The enemy is cruel, and we have to strike him where it will hurt him most. We must, Ihsan."

The young man regarded Shajar unhappily. It was as if he were seeing a side of her he had never seen before. "You wouldn't mind?" he asked.

"I wouldn't like doing it, but if it weren't necessary, I wouldn't be ordered to," Shajar replied.

She wondered if she loved Ihsan. Certainly she liked him in a way she had never liked anyone else. With the others in the camp she enjoyed at best an easy camaraderie, but she could talk to him about things which before she had always kept to herself, since those far-off days at the university. Nevertheless, this evening he had revealed a streak of weakness that worried her.

She had been so keen to give up her studies and fight, and her mother had encouraged her. Although she had never said so, Shajar suspected sometimes that her mother secretly hoped she would be killed fighting so that she would be ensured of eternal happiness. She enjoyed her training, but after a few weeks at Al Faktum she had begun to hate the camp itself with its national cliques and jealousies. Now that she must go, however, mixed with her excitement there was regret. She wondered if her reluctance to leave had something to do with Ihsan. If so, it was a weakness, and she must tolerate no weakness in herself.

"I'm leaving tomorrow," she said.

The young man looked at her, startled and concerned. "But your course isn't finished yet," he protested.

"It would have been in a few days, and they say I'm ready. Somebody is needed for a job, and I am to go."

"Where?"

"I don't know. I asked, but they said they would tell me tomorrow, just before I leave."

Ihsan felt that in some way he didn't altogether understand he was being betrayed. "How long have you known?" he demanded.

"Only this evening," Shajar answered.

He wanted to tell her she couldn't go, that she must try to get the order revoked. But he knew it would be useless, she was more dedicated than he was. He envied her and the rest their certainty more than anything else.

"Are you glad?" he asked.

"Of course I am." Shajar avoided his eye. "It's what I joined the army for. What I've been training for all this time. Now I'm to be of some use. Don't you envy me, Ihsan?"

TWELVE

Janet looked better today, Lorimer thought. As if, now the cremation was over, she could face starting a new life. She was wearing a cool summer dress and white sandals and more make-up than he had seen her use before. The cosmetics and her big white plastic earrings looked like a challenge, or, perhaps, an assertion of her independence.

There was no sign of Juliet or Stephen.

"Oh, it's you," she said. While her manner wasn't actively hostile, Lorimer had seen the slight frown that shadowed her face for a moment when she opened the door and found him in the porch. Clearly his presence wasn't welcome.

"I'm sorry, I have to see you," he told her.

"Why?"

"There are some things I have to ask you."

"I don't want to talk to you. I'm sorry, Gray, just go away. Please."

"It won't do any good," Lorimer said. "You know that."

Janet hesitated. "All right, come in," she agreed at last reluctantly.

She led the way into the room where they had talked before, and sat on the sofa. Lorimer sat in the chair he had taken then. Looking at Janet, he was convinced she was still afraid, but with the passing of the days her fear was losing its edge, so that now it no longer dominated her life, and she could forget it for hours at a time.

"How are you?" he asked.

She shrugged, not looking at him. "I'm all right."

"Are you on your own?"

"No. The children have gone to stay with my sister and her husband, but my mother's here. She's gone into the village to do some shopping this morning." Janet paused, then went on in a slight rush, "I'm sorry Stephen rang Jim Forster. He didn't need to; he didn't understand. He thought he was protecting me."

Despite her apologizing for him, she was proud of Stephen, Lorimer thought. If she wasn't careful, she would have a spoilt, arrogant young lout with a public-school accent for a son.

"It didn't matter," he said.

"Why have you come?" Janet wanted to know. His being there worried her, she looked nervous and on edge. "Last time you tried to tell me Mike was murdered."

"The police in Dhartoum showed me a wound on his head," Lorimer told her. "It couldn't have been self-inflicted."

"I don't understand."

"Don't you? He was coshed before he was put in the car and the pipe was connected to the exhaust. You've known all along he didn't commit suicide, yet you've gone on pretending he did, and you've let Juliet and Stephen believe it. Why?"

"That's a terrible thing to say."

"It's a terrible thing to do."

They stared at each other, angry and bitter.

Janet looked away first. "Why should I?" she muttered.

"Because you're frightened. Not as much as you were in Dhartoum, but you still can't be sure you're safe, even here."

She fumbled in a packet for a cigarette. "You're still talking about that, and it isn't true. I'm not frightened."

"How many are you smoking a day just now? Thirty?" Lorimer watched her take out a cigarette with trembling fingers, put it in her mouth and light it. "I don't blame you, you have plenty to be scared about."

"I don't know what you mean." Janet's voice rose. "I don't know anything."

"Why don't you stop lying?"

"How dare you!"

"All right," Lorimer said. If he had to bully her to learn the truth, he would. He must know. Not merely for his own satisfaction, not even because he was probably in danger too, but because too much was at risk to be squeamish about the feelings of one silly woman. "Out there that first evening you told me that neither of you had any money of your own. So how could you afford this house?"

"What business is that of yours?"

"I suppose you got a mortgage to buy it?"

"Yes, we did."

"Mortgages have to be repaid. You have two children at expensive schools, you ran two cars, and you dress well. All right, Mike may have taken out policies to provide for school fees, and his car belonged to the firm; it's still quite a life-style for somebody on eighteen thousand pounds a year and a few perks."

"We've always lived above our income," Janet said defiantly. "We're overdrawn at the bank, and we owe a lot on our credit cards. At least, I do, and Mike did."

They might, but that didn't account for half of it. O'Brien must have been paid well to persuade him to take the risks he had.

"What was he doing in Shajiha?" Lorimer asked.

"You know. He went to visit the office in Dhartoum. He went to all Maxwells' offices abroad."

"Not six times in less than two years."

"He said there were problems in Dhartoum."

"There were, but they weren't anything to do with Maxwells. Whose idea was it you went with him this time? His or yours?"

"His. I didn't want to go." Janet stubbed out her cigarette with quick, nervous movements. "We paid my fares and everything, there was nothing wrong in it."

"He'd never taken you before, and it wasn't as if you couldn't bear to be apart, was it? Didn't you wonder why he wanted you along if he was only going to sort out a problem at the office?" She was no fool; she must have realized there was more to his trip than some internal difficulty of Maxwells'.

"No," Janet said. "Why should I?"

"Because you knew what he was really doing out there. What he was being paid for—smuggling men from the camp at Al Faktum out of Shajiha."

Janet seemed to shrink a little. "It's not a crime to help political prisoners escape. They think you're a hero."

"Not in Shajiha." It was strange she should tell him the same story Hassan had done. Lorimer thought. But perhaps it was the cover for the camp. "Is that what he told you he was doing?" he asked.

"What do you mean?"

Janet looked puzzled, and Lorimer believed she hadn't known the truth. He was sorry for her. She might not have loved her husband very much, but still it would be a shock when she learned what he had really been doing in Shajiha.

"They weren't political prisoners," he told her. "They were terrorists—IRA, Red Brigades, ETA."

Janet stared at him, her eyes wide with horror and disbelief. "He wouldn't," she breathed. "Mike would never have done that."

"I'm sorry. The police know."

"You're wrong. It's just not possible."

"I've had the Special Branch or M.I.5 come to see me. They told me about Al Faktum. It's a training camp for top terrorists. When they leave there, they have to be smuggled out of Shajiha to their own countries. The immigration people have the ports and airports pretty well sewn up these days, so Mike shipped them out as members of the crew of one of Maxwells' ships. When they got where they were going, they disappeared ashore."

"You said the IRA," Janet told Lorimer. "She seemed suddenly to have gained confidence from somewhere.

"Amongst others. Terrorist groups all over the world send men to Al Faktum."

"Mike hated the IRA. He loathed them; they murdered his brother in Ulster. Pat was coming out of church with his wife and his two little girls, and they gunned him down in cold blood. They said afterwards they'd mistaken him for somebody else, as if that excused them. I'd never seen Mike like he was when it happened, he nearly went berserk."

Lorimer eyed her thoughtfully. The assurance with which she had spoken had shaken him at first, but perhaps it explained something that was puzzling him. "What happened when he came back the night before he was killed?" he asked.

Janet didn't answer at once. She was trying desperately to remember as much as she could. Getting it right mattered as much to her as to Lorimer.

"It was very late," she said. "Much later than he'd thought he'd be. I was worried. I believed he was helping prisoners to escape, and that if he was caught, anything might happen to him. To me, too. Then he came in. He looked dreadful. I asked him what was the matter, and why he was so late, but he wouldn't tell me anything, just said go into the bathroom and have a bath. I told him I'd had one while he was out, and he said, 'Have another one then. For God's sake, do what I say, Janet.' I thought he'd gone mad, that the heat had affected him or something."

Janet took another cigarette from the packet and toyed with it, twisting it in her fingers without lighting it. She seemed unaware of what she was doing. "I went into the bathroom and turned the water on. Then I heard the phone tinkle, and I guessed he'd wanted me out of the way while he called somebody. I expect he thought the sound of the water gushing into the bath would drown what he was saying. I couldn't believe it was happening. It was so unreal, like a story."

"Did you hear anything?" Lorimer asked.

"No. I didn't want to. Except I could hear he started by shouting at whoever he called. Then he seemed to cool down, I didn't hear him at all. Then the phone tinkled again as I got out of the bath and dried myself."

"Was it a long call?"

"I don't know. About six or seven minutes, I suppose, but it may have been ten." Janet looked at the mangled cigarette she was holding and dropped it into the ashtray, wiping the tips of her fingers together. "When I went back into the bedroom he was calmer, and I thought, whatever it was, the person he'd spoken to must have told him not to worry, it would be all right."

Lorimer thought it more likely they had arranged to meet him on the headland the following evening, but he didn't say so. Instead he asked, "Did either of you make any long-distance calls from the hotel?"

"I didn't—and I'm sure Mike didn't either. Why?"

"Nothing," Lorimer told her. "It doesn't matter. When did he tell you he was smuggling prisoners out of Shajiha?"

"When he wanted me to go out with him and I said I wouldn't. He'd never asked me to go anywhere before, places I'd have loved to go like Canada and Australia, and I didn't want to go to Shajiha. I suppose you wonder why not?"

"Why should you? It's hot and humid, and you thought it would be boring. You don't like flying, either."

Janet shook her head. "Partly, but it wasn't really any of those; I just didn't want to be with him when I didn't have to. I didn't love him any more, and when we were together we argued most of the time. I used to look forward to him going away." Her voice broke. "Now I just wish he was back. And I don't believe what you say. He wasn't bad, he wouldn't have taken money to help people like that."

Lorimer reflected that there was no telling what people would do if they were subjected to enough pressure. You only had to read the papers to learn of men who had yielded to coercion of one sort or another and ended up in gaol. Why should O'Brien be different? He suspected that Janet's defence of him owed something to her own feelings of guilt.

"I'm afraid there's no doubt about it," he told her. "I'm sorry, Janet."

"Inspector Mahfuz told me he knew what Mike had been doing. I thought he meant smuggling out prisoners. He said that if he'd been arrested and found guilty, he would have gone to prison for a very long time. He might even have been shot. Knowing what I did might be dangerous for me because there were people who could think I knew too much; I should keep quiet and say nothing about anything that had happened. I've been terrified."

Lorimer wondered what Mahfuz's role was. He suspected it was bigger and more involved than he had thought until now, and he remembered Hassan's warning not to underestimate the other Inspector.

"You say Mike looked dreadful when he got back to the hotel that night," he said. "Didn't he say anything at all about what had happened?"

"Just that it was all a bloody shambles and he'd been lied to all along the line. And there was something about the man he'd picked up, that he'd never make it. I asked him what he meant, and he told me not to worry him, he'd had as much as he could stand. The guards at the camp had seen him and fired at him." Janet stopped. Outside in the garden a thrush was singing, but here indoors it was very quiet.

Had he got it all wrong? Lorimer wondered. It didn't make sense.

"You know what I feel like doing?" Janet asked him. It was as if by telling him she had purged herself of some of her cares, and now there was a new light in her eyes.

"What?"

"Going out and getting very drunk."

"Why not? If that's what you want to do."

She shook her head. "It's not really, I'd only end up with a terrible head, and feel worse than ever. I've never been into a pub alone, and I don't think it would be very sensible to start now; I might find I liked going."

Lorimer stood up, and she followed suit, walking round the little coffee-table.

"I suppose it's better to know the truth," she said doubtfully.

"He may not have understood what he was doing," Lorimer told her. "Perhaps he really believed they were political prisoners he was getting out."

"Are you saying that just to be kind?"

"No."

"It makes it easier to believe. Thank you for coming, Gray." Janet put her hands on his shoulders and kissed him unhurriedly.

Lorimer felt her body, firm but yielding against his, and the light pressure of her lips. Her perfume was fresh and light in his nostrils.

"Oh God!" she breathed. "I'm so lonely." For a moment she clung to him almost desperately, then she moved away and said brightly, "Sorry."

"What for?" Lorimer asked. Pity had wiped out his dislike of Janet, but there was nothing he could do to help her.

"You know, blast you." She gave an unsteady little laugh.

She let him out and stood in the porch watching him walk across the gravel to his car, get in and start down the drive. When he turned into the lane, she sighed and went back indoors.

When Lorimer got back to United's offices, Borrett was out at a meeting. He unlocked a drawer of his desk and took out the file that contained the odds and ends he had brought back from Dhartoum. Amongst them was the O'Briens' hotel bill; so much had happened during the last few days, he hadn't got round to passing it on to Maxwells' accounts department. He took it out now and studied it. One item interested him particularly; his memory hadn't played him false.

In Shajiha it was just after four-thirty, and with luck Oldfield would be in the office. Lorimer looked up the number and the international dialling code, picked up his phone, and asked the operator for an outside line.

The Dhartoum manager sounded worried at hearing from him. "There's nothing wrong, is there?" he inquired anxiously.

"No," Lorimer lied. "I just want you to check something for me if you will. Accounts are querying O'Brien's expenses." He explained what he wanted. "It's not important, but if you could give me a ring as soon as possible, I'd be grateful. Then I can get them off my back. Don't talk to anybody else here. There are so many people in this place, ten to one I'd never get the message."

"All right," Oldfield agreed, his relief apparent even over the phone. "That won't be any trouble. Anything I can do."

"Thanks," Lorimer said.

He hung up and started on the backlog of work that had accumulated during his absence.

Borrett still hadn't returned when he left. On his way home he paused as usual at the bookstall at Victoria to buy an evening paper. The headline proclaimed PRESIDENT'S VISIT. DETAILS. The American President and his wife were starting a visit to Britain next Monday. Nominally it was a private trip, but on Tuesday the President would be addressing both Houses of Parliament, and some streets in Westminster and the West End would be closed temporarily. Lorimer folded the paper and went down to the District Line platform; the visit was unlikely to affect him.

Today there was no Melissa waiting when he entered his flat, and throwing his case and the paper onto the sofa, he went to wash and change. While he did so he debated whether to get himself a meal or go out. He didn't feel like taking the trouble to cook anything, but neither was the prospect of eating out alone very appealing. In the end he grilled a steak from the freezer and opened a bottle of supermarket Roussillon.

While he ate he studied the list of the *Maxwell Pride*'s sailings Oldfield had prepared for him. The first had left Dhartoum on April 4, 1983, for Genoa, Naples and Marseilles. The next, four and a half months later, had taken her to Alexandria, Marseilles and Bordeaux. Since then she had called at Bilbao, Tripoli in Lebanon, Piraeus and a number of other ports.

According to Lyddon, one of the extra hands she had taken on in Dhartoum, an Italian, had jumped ship in Genoa, a Spaniard had been left behind in Bilbao, and two Arabs had disappeared when the

ship called at Piraeus. On this last voyage she had been going to take
on yet another extra man. Possibly there had been others Lyddon had
forgotten, or simply not bothered to mention.

Genoa was close to the industrial cities of northern Italy where the
Red Brigades were most active, Bilbao in the Basque region, and
Tripoli in a country that in February 1984 had been on the brink of
civil war. Piraeus was the port of Athens, and there had been a number of terrorist bombings in Greece over the last two or three years.

Lorimer studied the list again. The *Maxwell Pride* had sailed from
Dhartoum for Piraeus on June 5, 1984. That meant she must have
arrived in the Greek port about the seventh of June. Christ! he
thought. For several seconds he sat, ignoring the food on his plate
while he considered the implications of his new idea. Then he got up,
went to the phone, and dialled Rosalind's number.

"You again!" she greeted him crushingly. "Aren't you out with your
friend of the sexy larynx tonight?"

"I'm sorry about that," Lorimer said. He told himself he didn't
have to apologize, it was no longer any affair of Rosalind's whom he
had in his flat.

"It's really of absolutely no interest to me," she said.

"Her name's Melissa. She's Jim Forster's daughter."

"My, my. First picked by the Chairman, now the MD's daughter."

Lorimer was on the point of saying he hardly knew her, but decided
that to do so would be both craven and untrue. Anyway, he didn't
owe Rosalind an explanation any more than an apology. "What date
was it we started back from the Dordogne last year?" he asked.

"You rang just to ask me that?"

"It's important, and women always remember dates better than
men."

"Lucky men," Rosalind commented tartly. Despite herself, she was
curious; Gray wasn't given to saying things mattered when they
didn't. "It was Friday, June 14. Why is it important?"

"I'll explain when I see you."

"Don't you mean *if?* Is that all you wanted?"

"Yes, thanks."

"I'll go back to my cheese salad then."

"Melissa eats like a horse," Lorimer said.

"She sounds as if she did," Rosalind commented unpleasantly. "Good night, Gray."

Grinning, Lorimer returned to his half-eaten steak. It was nearly cold, and the warmed-up frozen peas were beginning to look distinctly unappetizing. He remembered the drive north from their rented cottage near Beynac as much as anything because they had had the radio on in the car and the news had been full of the TWA Flight 847 hijacked en route from Athens to Rome. It was believed at the time that the Arab hijackers had boarded the plane at Athens airport. That was on the fourteenth, just a week after the *Maxwell Pride* had docked at Piraeus and two Arabs who joined the crew in Dhartoum jumped ship.

Jenkins had said Al Faktum was a training base for the operational elite of the terrorist world. Such men would only be employed on important missions, they were too valuable to be risked on minor "incidents." Missions like hijacking the TWA Boeing. Allow a few days in Athens for the operation to be set up, and the timing was right.

It was too late to check today whether there had been any major terrorist crimes committed in Spain and Italy after the *Maxwell Pride* docked in Bilbao and Genoa; that would have to wait until tomorrow, but in the meantime . . .

O'Brien had been in a position to arrange cargoes for the ports where men were to be taken, thus providing cover for the real purpose of the *Maxwell Pride*'s calling there. On her latest voyage she had docked at Alexandria and Marseilles. There had been no reports of any serious incident in Egypt or France recently, and it would probably have been unnecessary to go to such lengths to smuggle a man into Egypt; that could have been accomplished much more simply by land. Lorimer believed he could rule out Marseilles; the ship appeared to call there on every voyage, and it was the ports where she had docked only once or twice that interested him.

Almost certainly it was Sullivan who was supposed to join the crew at Dhartoum. The same Sullivan who was an officer in the IRA. And the *Maxwell Pride* hadn't called anywhere in Ireland, north or south, she had sailed straight home from the Mediterranean. Home to a port not two hours' travelling time from London.

Lorimer reached for the wine bottle. As he did so, out of the corner of his eye he saw the front page of the *Standard* he had tossed on the sofa with his briefcase when he came in. He stared at it, his hand still outstretched.

"Come out to the terrace," Grantley said, turning and leading the way through the house. "I asked Jim Forster to come, too. If what you have to say concerns Maxwells, he should hear it."

Lorimer would have much preferred to see the Chairman alone. He suspected that Forster's presence might well make a difficult discussion even trickier, but if that was what Grantley wanted, there was nothing he could do about it. He wondered if Forster had carried out his threat to tell the Chairman about Stephen O'Brien's complaint.

Maxwells' Managing Director was sitting in a teak chair. When the two men emerged from the house he looked at Lorimer and nodded coldly.

"Sit down," Grantley said. Lorimer obeyed. "You said on the phone what you had to say was urgent."

It might have been merely a statement of fact and an enjoinder to get down to business, but the implied threat was there none the less; this was Grantley's home, it was Saturday, and you invaded his privacy at your peril.

The small Georgian manor-house looked out across sloping gardens and a wide sweep of the Kent and Sussex countryside to the hazy outline of The Downs. Terrorism, violence of any sort seemed far away.

"I think it's urgent," Lorimer said, then added wryly, "I wouldn't have rung you on a Saturday if it wasn't."

Grantley smiled a shade grimly. "I hope not," he agreed.

"I went back to see Janet O'Brien yesterday."

The silence was like an icy pool. Lorimer waited for the Chairman to drop something into it, but Grantley only sat watching him. It was impossible to tell what he was thinking. Forster was waiting too, his eyes alert.

"I assume you had a reason for going?" Grantley said at last.

"Several. I was wrong about what O'Brien was doing: They weren't political prisoners he was smuggling out of Shajiha, they were terrorists."

Somewhere in the woods beside the house a pigeon cooed its plaintive, repetitive call, but none of the men on the terrace heard it. A new tension had come into the atmosphere.

"I don't believe it," Forster said harshly. "This is another of your ridiculous ideas."

Lorimer ignored him. "The camp at Al Faktum isn't a prison," he said, "it's a training camp for guerrillas. If you think I'm making it up, ask Jenkins, one of the M.I.5 men who came to my flat on Wednesday night, or Hassan's tutor at Cambridge, Humphrey Downing."

"Go on," Grantley told him.

"O'Brien's job was to get the terrorists out of Shajiha to the countries where they were to operate. I don't think he knew what they were, he was told they were political prisoners who had escaped, and he believed it. From what I've heard, he was a bit naive outside his job, and he needed the money he was paid. He and his wife couldn't have lived as they did on his salary from Maxwells, and neither of them had any money of their own."

"I've seen their house," Forster said. "But I still don't believe Mike O'Brien would do anything like that."

Grantley ignored him.

"Every time he visited the Dhartoum office, the *Maxwell Pride* docked there and he arranged for her to take on one or two extra hands," Lorimer went on. "I've talked to one of her officers. They didn't need any more crew, but they were told the office had arranged for the men to join them and they accepted it. When they got to their destinations the men either jumped ship or went sick and were left behind. I believe they were the men O'Brien smuggled out. The night before he was killed he drove out to Al Faktum to meet a man and drive him back to Dhartoum. Only something went wrong. Maybe he didn't obey the orders he'd been given; whatever it was, they were fired on by the guards at the camp."

Lorimer paused. "The man who was supposed to join the *Maxwell Pride*'s crew before she sailed never turned up. The next evening, O'Brien was killed, and the day after, another man's body was washed up not far from the headland where he was found. His name was Sullivan, he was an officer in the IRA. His skull had been smashed in."

Forster leaned forward in his chair. "You think he was the man

Mike went to meet, and the same people murdered them both?" he asked.

Lorimer shook his head. "No," he said. "I think O'Brien killed him."

THIRTEEN

The tension had increased. The two older men gazed at Lorimer in silence. Then Grantley demanded, "Have you any proof?"

"Not proof, no. But everything points to it. O'Brien had an Ulster accent; his wife told me. When he spoke, knowing he'd come to help him get out of the country, Sullivan would take it for granted he was an IRA sympathizer, and he'd talk. Not much, maybe, but enough for O'Brien to realize what he was. O'Brien loathed the IRA, they killed his younger brother in front of his wife and children when they were coming out of church a few years ago. You can guess how he felt when he saw he was being used to help them and people like them.

"He was late getting back to his hotel that night, and when he did he was in a terrible state. His wife thought the heat had affected his brain. He made her have a bath while he made a phone call so that she wouldn't hear who he was talking to or what he said. All he told her was that he'd been lied to all along the line, it was a shambles, and that the man he'd gone to pick up wouldn't make it. She didn't know what he was talking about."

"Do you know who he rang?" Forster inquired.

"No. But the call was on their phone bill and Oldfield's checking to see if the Carlton keep a record of numbers. He's ringing me on Monday. When Mrs. O'Brien came out of the bathroom, O'Brien seemed calmer. He'd probably been told to meet whoever he rang on the headland the next evening and they'd sort things out. When he went, they killed him."

"This man Sullivan, who told you about him?" Grantley asked.

"Ahmad Hassan first, then Jenkins."

"Inspector Hassan seems to have confided in you a lot," Forster commented.

He had, Lorimer thought. But not quite enough. Just as he hadn't trusted him enough. It was hot on the terrace and he was unaccustomed to talking so much; he would have liked a long cool drink. But clearly Grantley's thoughts were concentrated on what he had heard, so he went on, "Hassan was brought up in Britain. His father worked for the BBC, and he went to Cambridge. His wife's English. He was a moderate, and he probably saw the camp and the people who run it as a threat to the sort of Shajiha he believed in. If so, he'd do his best to get it closed down. I think that's why he was murdered."

"You think!" Forster said sarcastically. "It's all too circumstantial. There's no proof O'Brien had anything to do with any terrorists, or that he killed this man Sullivan."

"It may not be proof, but there's a lot of evidence," Lorimer retorted. He was determined not to be steam-rollered by Forster. "You can't just ignore it."

"Why not?" Forster looked at Grantley for support, but the Chairman was gazing into the distance, his face devoid of any expression. "Even if Mike did kill him, he's dead too now. There's nothing anybody can do."

Still Grantley said nothing. He doesn't want to know, Lorimer thought bitterly. He's like Forster. That two men are dead and I was bloody nearly killed is unfortunate, but it doesn't really matter. All they care about is sweeping the whole business under the carpet before it sullies United's good name and makes difficulties for the Group in the Middle East.

He was wrong. The Chairman was reflecting that Lorimer hadn't been afraid to disregard his instructions to forget about O'Brien when he saw a compelling reason for doing so. He had made his own decisions, not hidden behind his orders and used them as an excuse for doing nothing. Very likely he was right about the O'Brien boy, too; Lorimer would always antagonize people with an exaggerated sense of their own importance. In the long run that was a shortcoming and he would have to overcome it, but now, properly used, it could be an asset. Managing him wouldn't be easy, but he hadn't been looking for anybody who was too compliant; the sort of man he wanted for his trouble-shooter was rarely easy to handle.

"All right, you've made out a case," he said. "It's not conclusive, but you may be right. You still haven't told us why you had to see me so urgently."

"At the beginning of April 1983, the *Maxwell Pride* took on an Italian," Lorimer told him. "On the fourth, she sailed for Genoa. When she got there he jumped ship. On the twelfth, the Red Brigades kidnapped a judge in Milan and murdered him; his body was found in the boot of a car in a multi-storey car park in Turin a fortnight later. That November it was a Spaniard. When the *Maxwell Pride* reached Bilbao, he claimed he was sick, and they left him behind there. A few days later one of Spain's top generals was shot by ETA gunmen forty miles from Bilbao." Lorimer paused. "O'Brien went out to Dhartoum again at the beginning of June last year. While he was there, the *Maxwell Pride* docked and he arranged for her to take on two Arabs as extra hands. On June 5, she sailed for Piraeus. When she docked there on the seventh or eighth, the Arabs disappeared, and on the fourteenth, the TWA Boeing was hijacked while it was flying from Athens to Rome. At the time it was thought the hijackers smuggled themselves on board at Athens airport. This last voyage she was supposed to take on another man, and Sullivan was an IRA officer. She docked here on Tuesday."

They stared at him.

"You think . . ." Forster began. He looked appalled.

"I don't think," Lorimer told him. "I don't know. All I'm saying is that there's too much of a pattern to ignore it. And that I'm afraid a major terrorist action is planned here in England during the next two or three days. Probably in London. That's why it's urgent. I have to see Jenkins. He's the only person I know in Special Branch or M.I.5, and he knows me. I could go to the police, but they would ask a lot of questions and do a lot of checking before they took any action. We haven't time."

"And you think I can arrange it," Grantley said.

"Can't you?"

The Chairman thought. He had contacts, some of them at a very high level, in Whitehall and Westminster. There were men he could talk to, some of them men he knew well, who would listen, and who might help, if he pushed them hard enough. But if he did, and all this turned out to be a mare's nest, some of his credibility would be lost, and with it some of his influence. That had to be a consideration, not from any regard for personal vanity, but because his influence was important to United.

It took him only a few seconds to make up his mind. He was prepared to use all the influence he possessed. The only question was on whom should he use it?

"I'll see what I can do," he promised. "You'd both better stay to lunch." Standing up, he turned to Lorimer. "Have you any idea what these people mean to do?"

"Yes," Lorimer said. "They're going to try to assassinate the President of the United States."

"You make it sound plausible," Jenkins said. "I'll give you that. Too bloody plausible."

Lorimer thought he seemed less sceptical than he had expected. The Welshman probably spent a lot of his time dealing with what to most people would have been almost unimaginable.

Once Grantley had made his phone call, it was surprising how short a time elapsed before Jenkins arrived. He was on the fifteenth tee on the Old Course at Sunningdale when the message reached him, and it seemed to concern him more that he and his partner had been three up, and close to losing, than that he looked like forfeiting the rest of his weekend. He was still wearing his golfing clothes; his other things were in a bag in the boot of his car, together with his clubs and golf shoes.

Grantley had left the two men in his study, a largish, snugly furnished room with two windows overlooking the terrace, and old maps on the walls between the tall bookcases. Forster hadn't been able to stay after lunch, he had an appointment in London.

"Can you think of a bigger target?" Lorimer asked.

"One or two. But I see what you mean. And there are quite a lot of people who wouldn't be sorry to see them succeed." Jenkins eyed Lorimer speculatively. "Have you any ideas about when they mean to try, or is that as far as you've gone?"

Lorimer ignored the possible irony; maybe Jenkins hadn't intended it. "On Monday morning they fly into Heathrow and are driven to the Ambassador's house in Regent's Park, right?" Jenkins nodded. "On Tuesday he goes to Westminster to address both Houses of Parliament. What does he do after that?"

"The conventional things—visits to American institutions over here, lunch with the Chamber of Commerce, a trip to places with family connections."

"I reckon it will be Tuesday morning on his way to or from Parliament. This is going to be a big operation, and they won't want it to fail. So it will be planned down to the last detail, as precisely as possible. That's why I think going there's more likely, the timing is firmer then than coming back; he could speak longer than expected, or stay talking to people."

"He'll be here four days," Jenkins pointed out. "Why pick on Tuesday, when there'll be most security?"

"Because that's when his movements are most certain and not likely to be changed at the last minute. Besides, killing him on his way to Parliament would make the impact even bigger, and that's what they want, isn't it? As much publicity as they can get? And to show they can strike anywhere?"

Jenkins nodded. He was still not wholly convinced. "Killing the President would cause an enormous outcry in the States," he objected. "Let alone the rest of the world. There'd be the hell of a backlash. Why should the IRA want to alienate American opinion? They still rely on supporters there for a lot of their funds; some of that money might dry up if they murdered him."

"They wouldn't," Lorimer said. "Hizbollah would. The Party of God."

"*What?*"

"It's going to be a joint operation. That's what you people have been talking about for a long time, isn't it? An unholy alliance of terrorist groups working together on big operations? There've been rumours they've done it before, but it's never really happened." Lorimer paused. "To the Shajihan Hizbollah, America is the number-one enemy after Israel, and to the IRA, we are top."

Jenkins nodded. He thought that he had heard a lot of crazy ideas, but this was one of the craziest. Could Lorimer be right? If so, it was a horrifying prospect.

"The IRA does not exactly like this President," Lorimer went on. "He's talked too much about cracking down on terrorism. Okay, part of that may be rhetoric, but it makes the climate more difficult for them, so they might not be too sorry to see him go, provided somebody else was blamed. Especially as it would be bound to cause friction between Britain and the USA. The Americans would say it was partly our fault, our security wasn't good enough, and there'd be some bad feeling for a time."

"They're pretty sensitive about their own security just now."

"Maybe, but it would still be fuel for the anti-British crowd over there."

"They'd do their best to make capital out of it," Jenkins agreed. "But you said it was an IRA man O'Brien was supposed to put aboard the *Maxwell Pride* in Dhartoum. Are you suggesting he was going to work for Hizbollah?"

"Not directly. I believe there are going to be two incidents, one worked by the IRA, the other by Hizbollah. The first is meant to be a diversion to keep the Anti-Terrorist Branch people busy while the second one goes ahead. And that's the big one."

"Hizbollah's."

"That's right."

"So what are the IRA going to do?"

"I don't know. Maybe a bomb at some army barracks. It could be anything."

"Or anywhere."

"In London, ay."

"Or not a bomb, a shooting. Or a demonstration."

"Not a demo," Lorimer said. "The ordinary police would deal with that, and the IRA will want to make a big show of their own as well as keeping the Anti-Terrorist men well away from Hizbollah's target area."

"So we haven't a bloody clue," Jenkins said.

"No."

"And while we're chasing about like a lot of blue-arsed flies, they shoot the President."

"They won't shoot him."

"Oh?" It was impossible to tell whether Jenkins meant that ironically.

Lorimer hesitated. If it had been tricky up to this point, from now on it would be doubly so. Jenkins might just laugh at him, and if he did, it meant the whole theory would go down the tubes. Nobody would pay attention to any of it. "A gun's not sure enough," he said.

"Do you know what the latest weapons can do?" Jenkins asked seriously. "They can shoot round bloody corners, man."

Lorimer moved restlessly. "Look," he said. "Over here we like to pretend we don't really need security. The Queen can ride in open carriages and walk through crowds, right? So security keeps a low profile. The Americans work the other way, they have to. They make a great show of strength to act as a deterrent. The car that takes the President to Westminster will be closed and bullet-proof, and guarded by a posse of Secret Service men. And it won't hang about."

Jenkins nodded. He wondered what Lorimer was getting at.

"So it wouldn't present much of a target for a marksman along the route. He'd hit the car, maybe, but he wouldn't have more than a fifty-fifty chance of killing the President. If that."

"That's the idea."

"And nobody could get near enough, or move fast enough to throw a bomb with any certainty of hitting the car."

"Except when he gets in and out of it."

"At the door of the Ambassador's house and right outside the door at the Houses of Parliament? Nobody would be allowed near enough."

"They were when they killed Mrs. Gandhi," Jenkins said.

Lorimer was startled. "You think one of the President's body-guards . . . ?"

"No, only that it happened then, so it's a possibility. Anyway, that's the Americans' concern, not ours." Jenkins eyed his companion curiously. "The side streets will be closed off, no parking will be allowed along the route, and there'll be other cars in front of the President's and behind it. If you're thinking of a suicide driver in a van loaded with explosives, forget it; he'd never get through."

"Not a driver," Lorimer said. "A pilot."

"A *what?*" It was Jenkins' turn to be startled.

"This operation has to succeed. I'm like you, I can't see any way they could do it on the ground and guarantee success. So they must plan to hit him from the air. That's another reason why it's almost certainly Hizbollah; they're glad to die for their cause, the IRA aren't. Not deliberately in cold blood."

"And you think they'll use a plane?"

"No, a helicopter. It's far more practical for that sort of operation."

"It'd be spotted and seen off before it got near its target."

"Would it when nobody was looking out for it? If it took off from somewhere in London, it wouldn't have to be airborne more than a few minutes, and even if somebody did become suspicious, there wouldn't be time to do anything."

"My God!" Jenkins muttered. "Are you seriously suggesting they mean to hijack a helicopter, load it with explosives and crash it on the President's car?"

"More likely they'll buy one," Lorimer replied. "If they tried to steal it, there'd be the risk of failure, and, even if they succeeded, there'd be a time-lag while they flew it to their hideaway and loaded it. They'd probably have to do it the day before, with everybody hunting them. Far simpler and safer to have their own. That way they needn't come out into the open until the last minute. The cost wouldn't be a factor, they have plenty of money."

"You've got it all worked out, haven't you?" Jenkins commented, masking his respect with irony.

Lorimer grinned. "They tried to kill me," he pointed out.

"So you have a vested interest in putting them away."

"It's not just that." It was all they stood for; the fanaticism and the blind arrogance that believed only they were right and the end justified whatever means they employed to achieve it; that was prepared to kill quite casually men, women and children whose only crime was that they happened to be there when one of their bloody bombs went off. It was Hassan and his wife, O'Brien and Janet, young Juliet with her sad eyes grieving for her father, and even Stephen, too.

Jenkins gave Lorimer a thoughtful look. "No, I don't suppose it is," he agreed.

"What are you going to do?"

"First I'll report what you've said."

"And then?"

"It'll be out of my hands."

For a moment neither man spoke. Both were thinking about what might happen when Jenkins talked to his superiors, very aware that, if they weren't convinced, nothing might be done.

"They can't have got it long ago," Lorimer said. "The makers must have records of the machines they've sold during the last three or four months."

"They may have bought it second-hand," Jenkins pointed out. Already he was talking as though he accepted Lorimer's theory, he thought. Perhaps subconsciously he did, while his conscious mind still had reservations.

"There can't be that many helicopters on the market at any one time," Lorimer objected. "And my bet is they'll have bought it in this country, shipping it here would cause too many complications."

"They could have flown it in."

"A helicopter hasn't a very long range, and you can't land a plane that's big enough to carry one in somebody's back field."

"Ireland isn't too far away, and France is nearer."

"If that's what they did," Lorimer said grimly, "it's just bloody bad luck. We'll never find it."

Jenkins ignored the implication that Lorimer would continue to be involved. "They won't have registered it," he observed.

"No."

They looked at each other, both of them reflecting that it was already Saturday afternoon. What were the odds against the helicopter's being discovered in time? If, indeed, it existed. Maybe they were on the wrong track, and the attack would come in some other way.

"It could be difficult getting hold of people at the makers today or tomorrow," Jenkins remarked, his tone deceptively casual.

"Yes," Lorimer said. "It must be in London or somewhere very close. The shorter the time it's in the air, the better from their point of view." Perhaps, he thought, the best hope of averting a disaster was in dealing with it once it was airborne. But that would be running things very, very tight.

"London's a big city," Jenkins commented. "And you don't need a lot of space to hide a chopper."

"Nor for it to take off and land. I know."

The Welshman straightened up as if he was preparing mentally for the task ahead; persuading his superiors to take Lorimer's ideas seriously wouldn't be easy. Just now, whether he was right or wrong didn't matter too much, it was action that was needed and getting it might be difficult.

"I'd better be going," he said. "There's quite a lot to do."

"Will you give me a number where I can contact you?" Lorimer asked. "Just in case something comes up."

Jenkins took his diary from his pocket and scribbled in it. Then, tearing out the page, he handed it to the younger man. "If we aren't in time, and anything happens, you'll know you were right," he said.

"I'll watch the news," Lorimer told him.

Jenkins walked to the door. "What will you do if you're wrong?" he asked.

"Look for another job." He had burnt his boats pretty comprehensively, Lorimer thought, and if he was wrong, he would be extremely unpopular in a lot of quarters. Maybe he had better emigrate. "Oldfield's ringing me back from Dhartoum on Monday," he said. "When he does, there's something else I want to ask him."

Jenkins looked as if he were going to ask what it was, then he changed his mind. "I'd be careful if I were you," he warned. He went out.

A few minutes later, when Lorimer passed an open window on his way to his car, he heard the Welshman on the telephone. He got into the Saab, drove slowly down the winding drive, and turned out into the main road.

It was still a beautiful day, there was little traffic, and in other circumstances he would have enjoyed the drive. As it was, putting his fears into words and having to justify them had served only to strengthen his conviction that he was right.

He tried to think about Melissa instead. It was less than a fortnight since their first meeting, yet already she was beginning to monopolize a part of his life. He hadn't expected that to happen, hadn't wanted it.

Beyond an elderly woman driving a Mini Metro at a sedate forty, the road was narrow, but without a bend for a good two hundred yards. Lorimer glanced in his rear-view mirror, ready to overtake. The only other vehicle in sight was another car seventy or eighty yards back. He pulled out.

As he did so, the other driver accelerated, sweeping past the Metro before pulling in again behind the Saab as they approached a right-hand bend.

Coming out of it, Lorimer glanced in his mirror again. It occurred to him that there was something familiar about the other car. But he must be mistaken. After all, there were plenty like it on the roads now. The driver had moved out a little, starting to overtake him.

Ahead, the road ran straight for at least a hundred and fifty yards before turning left round the head of a deep valley. A white-painted wooden fence guarded the edge on that side, while on the right the hillside rose steeply almost from the edge of the tarmac.

Lorimer could see right round the bend to the far side of the valley. There was nothing coming towards them, and he kept well over to give the other driver plenty of room to pass.

The car edged up alongside. As it did so, Lorimer had a sudden vision of the Mercedes pulling up beside his taxi on the road into Dhartoum, the gun protruding from its rear window and, behind it, the face of Saad Hatem. But this car wasn't a Mercedes, and the driver was alone. He was wearing a light-coloured jacket like a wind-cheater, its collar turned up, and an American-style gold cap with a visor. Together they effectively concealed his head and shoulders. A man on his way home after a Saturday-morning round at his club, that was all. Yet Lorimer had a sudden shocking presentiment of danger.

Already the car was almost past. He braked hard. By the time the other driver saw what he had done, it was twenty yards ahead. He slowed too, and Lorimer's last doubts vanished.

A second more and the two cars were abreast again, less than eighteen inches between them. On the Saab's other side the fence was only a foot away, with beyond it a steep drop of two hundred feet to the floor of the valley. The other car was crowding the Saab, forcing it towards the edge of the road. The fence might look solid, but Lorimer could see it was only a rail-and-post affair. A car striking it at speed would snap it like a twig.

Already the Saab's near-side wheels were scrabbling in the dust outside the asphalt. The space was just wide enough. Jaw set, Lorimer shoved his foot hard down on the accelerator. The Turbo surged forward.

But even as it did so the other car edged in farther, narrowing the gap. The Saab struck it just behind its front-wheel arch with a shriek of tearing metal. Cannoning off the bigger car, it crashed into the fence between two of the upright posts. The single rail snapped. Lorimer saw the other car veer across the road as the driver struggled to control it, then the Saab was falling sideways through the gap in the fence.

Time seemed to slow eerily. It could have been only a second or two before the car hit the ground, but it felt much longer. When it did, bodywork crunched. Lorimer was jerked violently by his seat-belt and the diagonal strap cut painfully into his right shoulder. The Saab bounced once. Then it began rolling over and over sideways, thudding sickeningly at each turn as it gathered speed down the steep slope.

Lorimer's head was swimming. How much longer could the Saab stand up to this remorseless pounding before it disintegrated altogether? It was falling over comparatively smooth turf, but already pieces of its bodywork were being torn away.

The rolling seemed to go on for a long time. Lorimer tried to remember what he had seen at the bottom of the valley, but his attention had been concentrated on the road and the other cars. If the Saab hit a wall or a tree at this speed, it would be smashed into a shapeless mass of metal with him inside it.

The next second there was a final crushing impact, far worse than any before, and it stopped. Despite his seat-belt, Lorimer felt as if he had been hurled against a stone wall by some huge catapult. His senses reeled and he was on the verge of losing consciousness. But the belt held him securely. At first the sudden cessation of the rolling over and over was as much of a shock as the spinning, but after a few seconds his head began to clear.

A pair of pigeons flew away with a great rustling of leaves, squawking in alarm. When they had gone, the stillness was almost uncanny. Through the windscreen Lorimer could see trees, straight beeches with greyish trunks, the sun shining obliquely between them brightening the carpet of brown leaves. Only the trees didn't grow upright, they pointed horizontally, and the ground wasn't where it should have been. Foliage, small bright green leaves, pressed against the windscreen. He realized that the car was lying on its side. It must have rolled into the edge of a wood where bushes had checked its speed so that the collision with a tree that finally stopped it, stunning though it was, was less devastating than it would have been otherwise.

The roof just behind the front seats had taken the worst of the impact, stoving it right in. A few inches to the right and the blow would have been just over his head. That would have been the end. Craning his neck, Lorimer looked out of the driver's window. There were no trees on that side, only the steep bare hillside climbing up to the road.

A new wave of faintness engulfed him and he felt a terrible lethargy. All he wanted was to remain there while he recovered some of his strength. But instinct told him he must get out. He shook his head to clear it, and wished he hadn't; a sharp pain shot through his temples. Forcing himself to take his time, he pressed the release catch on his seat-belt.

Free of the belt, he turned and tried to open the door. Nothing happened. The lock was jammed. Try as he might, he couldn't open it. With the car lying on its other side and the roof crushed in, there was no other way out. If he couldn't open the door, he was trapped.

Until that moment he had acted almost automatically, hardly thinking about what he was doing, but now he smelt something. At first the odour was very faint, but it became stronger every second. Petrol. Recognition brought a new and greater fear. A fuel pipe must have been damaged in that last crushing impact when the Saab hit the tree. Or perhaps the tank had split. He had filled it at a service station only a few miles from Grantley's house that morning, it must be nearly full. If petrol leaked onto the hot engine . . .

For as long as he could remember Lorimer had had a secret horror of being trapped in a fire, unable to escape. When he was a child, it had been his home that was ablaze. As he grew older, it became a plane or a car. These days he hardly thought about it. Now that fear returned, more real, more terrifying than ever before. He began to struggle desperately with the door.

FOURTEEN

Jenkins was ringing the duty officer at Headquarters when Lorimer left. His call finished, he said goodbye to Grantley and set off for London.

When he first saw the Metro parked rather too close to a bend on a narrow stretch of the road he thought something uncomplimentary about its driver. The road ahead was clear right round the bend, and he glanced in his mirror before pulling out to pass it. Then he saw a woman waving to him and, behind her, a long gap in the fence bordering the road. Another car was parked a little farther on.

Some poor devil had gone through the fence, he supposed. He was in a hurry to get to his office. Whether Lorimer was right or not, there was a great deal to be done, and somebody else was already on the spot here. Nevertheless that broken fence looked ominous, and another few minutes was unlikely to make any difference. Braking, he pulled up just past the Metro.

The woman came hurrying up before he had time to get out, panting and looking very distressed. She was at least seventy.

"A car went down there," she gasped, pointing with an unsteady hand down the slope. "You can see it—or what's left of it. There against the trees. It was frightful, the other car went right into it."

Jenkins looked and saw the car at the edge of the wood. He felt a sudden sense of foreboding. It was what she had said about another car hitting it, her tone almost suggesting the other driver had caused the crash deliberately.

"Was it that car there hit it?" he asked, nodding at the one parked just along the road. Surely not, there were no signs of damage to it.

"No, no. Another one."

"You mean it looked as if the driver meant to force it off the road?"

She turned faded, intelligent eyes on him. "It sounds so unlikely, doesn't it? But it did look like that. He cut right across that car down there before he was really past it. I was following them and I saw what happened."

She was probably imagining it, Jenkins thought. On the other hand . . .

"What about that man?" he asked, indicating the other car again.

"He said he was going to see if there was anything he could do."

Jenkins reached into his car for the tyre lever he kept there. It had come in useful more than once before, although not for the purpose for which it was intended. "Could you find a telephone and ring for an ambulance?" he asked.

"I was going to when I saw you coming," the old lady replied.

Jenkins lowered himself through the gap in the fence. The leather soles of his shoes gave no grip on the dry turf and he slithered down the slope. More than once he fell. But he was anxious now. Lorimer had been only a few minutes ahead of him, and he would have driven along this road.

When he was still some distance from it he could see that the car was so badly damaged as to be unrecognizable. But it was black, and Lorimer's Saab was black. Another few yards and he could smell the familiar sickly stench of petrol. "Oh, Christ!" he prayed.

A man was bending over the wreckage, peering in at one of the windows. As the Welshman approached he looked up.

"You!" Jenkins exclaimed.

When the door wouldn't open, Lorimer tried again and again to force the lock. Nothing happened. Already the stink of escaping petrol was nauseating. He had to get out, and get out quickly. His head swimming again, he made himself concentrate on the door. That way he didn't think so much about the petrol and what would happen when the vapour reached the hot engine.

The lock and the driver's window were both jammed, and he had nothing with which to smash the toughened glass, but where the door hinges were attached to it, the Saab's bodywork was twisted. If he could apply enough pressure there, just possibly the hinges would tear free. It was an outside chance, but he couldn't see anything else.

With the roof partly stoved in, moving was difficult, but he managed to twist round so that his shoulders were braced against the other door. The position was cramped and acutely uncomfortable, but he hardly noticed that; now he could push with his feet against the driver's door.

At first nothing moved. Desperately he tried again, using all the strength of his leg and back muscles. And this time metal creaked protestingly. Sweat stood out on his forehead and ran down his face. He pushed again, straining every sinew, nearly overcome by the physical effort and the fumes in that confined space.

When a face appeared at the window, he told himself he was imagining it. He must be. What could Muhammad Ghanim be doing here? Unless it was the Shajihan who had forced him off the road.

Lorimer's head felt as if it were stuffed with cotton wool. The strength had deserted his legs and he couldn't push any more. If only he weren't so faint . . . Then weakness seemed to envelop him and he passed out.

When Jenkins arrived on the scene a few seconds later, Ghanim was wrestling with the door handle.

"He is in there," he said.

The Welshman set to work with his tyre lever. It took only moments to open the door, and together they lifted Lorimer out.

"We'd better get him into the wood," Jenkins said. "She'll go up any minute."

Between them the two men carried Lorimer's limp form through the trees until they were a good hundred yards from the car. There they lowered him to the ground.

"Let's hope that's far enough," Jenkins commented.

Even as he spoke there was a great sighing roar as the Saab's petrol tank exploded. They felt the hot blast of air on their faces. Within seconds the car was an inferno. The searing heat scorched the trees and devoured the bushes, sending showers of charred and burning leaves high into the air. Birds flew out, screeching in alarm, but the noise of the flames drowned their cries.

"God!" Jenkins breathed. He turned back to Lorimer.

"He is all right?" Ghanim asked.

"I think so."

As if to confirm the Welshman's opinion, Lorimer stirred. His eyes opened for a moment, then closed again.

"He is one of yours?"

"No." Jenkins straightened up. "How did you come to be on the scene so promptly?"

The Shajihan ignored the question. "If he is not one of yours, perhaps he is one of theirs," he suggested.

"Not that either. He's just an innocent bystander."

Ghanim gave Jenkins a very straight look, then he shrugged. "In that case he is unfortunate," he commented.

"You've been watching him. You thought he was involved in the Al Faktum business, and that he might have killed your man Hassan."

"It was possible."

"He wasn't and he didn't. The last thing he wanted was Hassan dead." Lorimer stirred again and Jenkins looked down at him. "Did you see who was driving the car that forced him off the road?" he asked.

"Only that it was a man," Ghanim replied.

Lorimer tried to sit up. After a moment, with Jenkins' help, he succeeded.

"Where am I?" he wanted to know.

"In the wood," the Welshman told him. He grinned. "You ought to drive more carefully, you made the hell of a mess of that fence."

Against Jenkins' advice, Lorimer refused to go to hospital in the ambulance for a check-up.

"How are you going to get home then?" Jenkins asked ironically. "It's several miles to the nearest station."

Ghanim had already departed in the red Sierra and the elderly woman in her Metro.

"You'll take me," Lorimer said. "Won't you?"

"Why should I? You ought to go to hospital, and you've given me plenty to get on with without acting as your chauffeur."

Lorimer thought of the last time he had been in a hospital, in Dhartoum, and feeling the cold dead flesh over O'Brien's injured skull. "I hate hospitals," he said.

"All right," Jenkins agreed. "I'll take you. But you'll have to wait while I make a call first."

He walked across to his car, slid into the passenger's seat, and closed the door behind him. Lorimer waited, looking down the slope to where he could see the twisted and blackened remains of the Saab.

He felt bitter and resentful. It might be absurd to feel like that about it when he had nearly been killed, but he had liked that car.

After two or three minutes Jenkins rejoined him.

"Right, let's go," he said, turning back to the Montego.

Lorimer got in beside him and he swung the car out onto the road, reflecting that it was fortunate the old girl in the Metro hadn't insisted on calling the police. He could have dealt with them, but inevitably that would have taken time they could ill afford.

"My section head wants to see you," he said.

"Why?" Lorimer asked.

"Probably to see what sort of nut you are."

"Thanks."

"Or maybe he just doesn't believe me."

Lorimer told himself he didn't want to see Jenkins' boss. He didn't want to see anybody; all he wanted was to go home to bed. If he had nine hours' sleep, he would be all right in the morning. But he knew he couldn't very well refuse, and that it was his own fault, he should have taken Jenkins' advice and gone to hospital.

The Welshman pushed his foot harder on the accelerator and the Montego surged past two other cars. If Lorimer was right, they had precious little time, he thought, and already nearly an hour had been wasted.

Heavy traffic in south London delayed them further, and when they reached Headquarters Lorimer was directed to a cloakroom to wash and tidy himself as best he could while Jenkins went to talk to Cowper, the head of his section.

"You think they were really trying to kill him?" Cowper asked.

"It looks like it."

"Why? Once he'd talked to you, it was a bit late to shut him up, surely?"

"They may not have known he'd talked to me," Jenkins said. "If they followed him to Grantley's place, and waited down the lane for him to leave, all they'd have seen was a car arriving. It might not have had anything to do with Lorimer or us."

Cowper looked doubtful. "Perhaps," he conceded.

"There's something else. Ghanim was there when I got to where Lorimer crashed. He was trying to get him out of the car."

"Interesting."

"He admitted he'd been keeping an eye on him."

"Did he?" Cowper picked up his phone. "Let's have Lorimer in."

The two men waited in silence until he came, escorted by a grey-haired secretary who departed as soon as she had shown him into the room.

"How do you feel now?" Cowper asked.

"I'll live."

"Good." Privately Cowper was surprised that Lorimer was still on his feet. He must be bloody sore, he thought. "I'm sorry to have to ask you to go through everything you told Owen Jenkins again, but I'd like to hear it from you," he said.

"To make sure I tell the same story?" Lorimer asked ironically.

"Partly. And partly so that I can form my own impressions without being influenced by what he's told me. Also, it's possible that this time we may see something he missed before."

"Where do you want me to start?"

"At the beginning, please."

It took some time, and more than once Cowper interrupted with questions Lorimer guessed were designed to test the truth of what he was saying as well as to clarify certain points in Cowper's mind.

"I'll have to talk to Sir Brian," the latter said when Lorimer had finished.

"Who's he?"

Cowper had been speaking to Jenkins, although he was still looking at Lorimer. "Sir Brian Wycliffe, our boss," he answered.

"Is he in today?" Jenkins asked.

"No. But I reckon he'll come in when he hears about this."

Cowper was right.

"I'll be there in half an hour," Wycliffe told him. "While you're waiting, get on to the Home Office and Grosvenor Square and tell them we may need to have a meeting at six."

"Do you want to see Lorimer?" Cowper inquired.

"What shape's he in?"

"A bit shaken up, otherwise he doesn't seem too bad. He's lucid enough."

There was a momentary pause. "Where does he live?" Wycliffe asked.

"South Kensington."

"Send him home to change and see to anything he wants to, then, and bring him back. I'll talk to him. Do you think there's anything in his story?"

"I don't know," Cowper admitted. "He's made out a pretty good case."

Wycliffe grunted. "You can make out a pretty good case for all sorts of rubbish if you've enough imagination," he commented.

It was less than thirty minutes before he arrived, a powerfully built, bluff-looking man with a tanned skin and a thatch of greying hair. His appearance was deceptive, his eyes were shrewd and his brain was reputed to be one of the keenest in public service. A senior civil servant, then an unusually young master of a Cambridge College before being picked by the Prime Minister for his present post, he had practical experience of both Whitehall and Westminster, and, it was rumoured, a pretty poor opinion of them both. He himself would have said that he understood their weaknesses as well as their strengths. His favourite recreations were golf and fell walking in his native Lake District, and his stamina was legendary. He moved quietly, without noise or fuss, but when he entered a room he brought with him, like an aura, the strength of his personality.

"What's Lorimer like?" he demanded, seating himself at his desk.

Cowper glanced at Jenkins, as if to say he knew him better.

"One of the quiet Scots," the Welshman said. "I shouldn't think he'd imagine anything like this, he seems to have his feet pretty firmly on the ground. And Sir Aidan Grantley must think well of him, he chose him to go out to Dhartoum."

"For a straightforward job almost anybody could have done." Wycliffe looked from Jenkins to his section head. "Or do you think Grantley suspected something was going on out there?"

"I doubt it," Cowper answered.

"I wonder. I know Grantley, he can be as devious as a politician when he wants to be."

"We had Lorimer checked out as soon as we heard from Humphrey Downing that he was showing a lot of interest in Hassan and the camp at Al Faktum," Jenkins remarked. "There was nothing to make us look twice at him."

"Meaning he doesn't write poetry, belong to a society for the protection of alien spacemen, or get himself arrested for importuning in public bogs," the Chief said. His opinion of security screenings was well known in the Service, and the two men smiled.

"So far everything we know bears him out," Jenkins commented. "I've talked to Franklin. The Anti-Terrorist Squad knew Sullivan; he was one of the IRA's up-and-coming hard men, part of their Belfast command. If Lorimer's right, he was probably the liaison between them and Hizbollah, and he was coming back to take charge of their end of the operation when he was killed. They'll have had to bring someone in to replace him at short notice. Franklin says one of their most experienced explosives men hasn't been seen in Belfast for the last few days." Jenkins stopped. "He told me something else, too. There are reports in Ulster that something big is planned for the next week or two, probably in London."

"There's another thing Lorimer doesn't know that ties in with his theory," Cowper added. "Two Shajihans flew in on Friday. They were supposed to be new staff for the embassy, but the people there say they know nothing about them and nobody's arrived."

For a few seconds Wycliffe sat immobile, considering what he had heard, then he turned to Cowper. "Get back to the Home Office," he said. "Tell them it's urgent and the meeting's on. Say I think the Home Secretary should be advised, and I don't want them sending along some under-under-under secretary with no power to decide anything. I'll talk to the Americans." Wycliffe had no false modesty where his own influence was concerned, he knew that if he said something was urgent, highly placed people would listen. Glancing up at the clock on the wall now, he added, "When I've spoken to them I'll see Lorimer. That will leave us half an hour to decide what we're going to ask for. Have you two any thoughts about that?"

"We've made a few notes," Cowper told him, pushing a sheet of paper across the desk. He stood up. "God help us if Lorimer's wrong."

Wycliffe regarded him sombrely. "And if he's right," he said.

Through the window in the wall facing him, Lorimer could see the roofs of the buildings across Whitehall and, above them, a single white cloud in an otherwise clear sky. He felt slightly overawed. Besides Wycliffe, seated with him round the table in the big, high-ceilinged room there were the Home Secretary, the American Ambassador, the deputy head of Scotland Yard's Anti-Terrorist Squad, an officer in the American Secret Service, a CIA man named Carpenter and the Minister's permanent private secretary. He wondered why Wycliffe had wanted him here. These men were professionals, used to dealing with the heads of governments, they wouldn't take any notice of him.

Wycliffe had had his own reasons for wanting Lorimer there. In a way the Scot was insurance. It was the Chief's way to cherish his own mental reservations, sacrificing them only when no further doubt remained, and he wasn't wholly convinced that Lorimer was right. At the same time, taken with what the Service already knew, his theory was credible enough to be taken seriously. Moreover, it counted with Wycliffe that Jenkins was eighty per cent convinced, he had considerable respect for the Welshman's judgement.

Wycliffe believed it was unlikely the Americans would take much persuading; it was their President whose life could be in danger and they had nothing to lose, but the Home Secretary might be a harder nut to crack. He wouldn't support the action Wycliffe was going to propose without being satisfied it was absolutely necessary. He could be as stubborn as a mule when he was so inclined, and his support was essential. Without it, the police could be in a very difficult position; they might even refuse to act.

Look at him now, Wycliffe thought. He's frowning because I've got him in a corner and he knows it. And he's worried about what the PM will say. Nevertheless, the Chief was confident that with the Americans leaning on him, and Lorimer to provide first-hand evidence if required, the Home Secretary would yield. He wouldn't dare take the risk inherent in refusing.

Most of the men round the table had been at home enjoying the fine Saturday afternoon when they were summoned to the meeting, and it was a tribute to Wycliffe's reputation that they had come with no more than token grumbling. The sense of expectation in the room while they waited for him to explain could almost be felt.

Lorimer heard him like through a haze. It was no longer only his head and shoulder, his whole body ached, and he found it hard to concentrate. The aspirins he had taken had had little effect, and he wondered how long it would be before he could go home again to bed.

"So there you are, gentlemen," Wycliffe concluded.

There was silence, as if nobody wanted to be the first to speak. Then the Home Secretary said in his rich voice, "Thank you, Brian. From what you've said, I assume you think we should take this seriously?" His glance flickered over Lorimer.

"Jesus Christ, we must!" Carpenter, the CIA man, sounded outraged. He was about Lorimer's age, lean, tough and humourless, with close-cropped hair and strangely remote blue eyes. Before being posted to the London station a month before, he had spent most of his service at Langley, and he was finding the transition difficult. The people over here, Americans as well as Limeys, didn't know a goddam thing. They were so laid back they were nearly on their asses, and to hear them talk you'd think the Reds didn't even exist. He'd like to have them back in Langley for a week, he'd show them what the world was all about.

Everybody was looking at him. "The President's life's in danger," he said violently.

"You accept that?" Wycliffe asked him.

"Too damned right I do."

"If it is, there are other things we have to consider."

"Other things? What, for God's sake?"

It was Harper, the Secret Service man, who answered. "Do you know what a helicopter loaded with explosives crashing into a street would do?" he asked. "Sir Brian's saying it's not only the President's life that's at risk, it's maybe a hundred, two hundred lives, British as well as American. Am I right, sir?"

Wycliffe nodded. "Yes," he agreed.

Carpenter was glaring at Harper. To Lorimer his expression seemed like that of a man whose detestation went deeper than mere personal dislike. Carpenter had no use for the Secret Service man, possibly for the Service itself, and Harper had put him in the wrong. But perhaps he was imagining it. If only he didn't feel so weak.

"Okay, okay," Carpenter said roughly. "But it's the President's concerns me. That's why we're here."

The Home Secretary was too experienced a politician to be embarrassed. "What action are you proposing, Brian?" he inquired.

"One, we're asking Westland and all the other helicopter manufacturers to supply us with lists of everybody they've sold machines to during the last four months," Wycliffe replied. "Second, we want every policeman and woman and every traffic warden in London and the Home Counties to be asked whether they've seen a helicopter on the ground, or taking off or landing, even just flying low, anywhere they wouldn't normally see one in the last three or four weeks. Third, we want the police to carry out a thorough ground and air search of that whole area to check on every place where a helicopter could be hidden. There are other steps, but those are the ones we see as immediate and essential."

The Home Secretary gazed at him, his expression blank. Damn Wycliffe! he thought. The man was a maverick, he had no sense of political responsibility at all. It was common knowledge that he wasn't above playing off Whitehall and Westminster against each other when it suited his purpose. It had been typically high-handed of him to demand this meeting. Why couldn't he have come to see him quietly without dragging the Americans and the Anti-Terrorist people into it? Time enough to bring them in after they had considered all the aspects. But of course he knew why; Wycliffe was trying to force his hand.

The search alone would require a small army, with men working overtime at a time when police overtime was supposed to be reduced. With a shudder the Home Secretary remembered the difficulties there had been over payments for policing the miners' strike. Moreover, inevitably some people would be upset, and there were bound to be questions in the House and the media about police powers and the cost at a time when public expenditure on essential services was being cut to the bone.

The Home Secretary picked up a pencil that was lying on his desk, toyed with it for a few seconds, then snapped it in his fingers. It broke with a sharp little crack, and he looked at the pieces as if he were surprised to see them there.

"A search like that will be an enormous undertaking," the deputy head of the Anti-Terrorist Squad said. "You reckon we've got just over forty-eight hours."

"That's if Lorimer's right and the attack is planned for Tuesday," Wycliffe told him. "It's possible they could strike on Monday."

"Or not at all," the Home Secretary said. "The whole thing is supposition; we don't know there's going to be an attack."

Carpenter was looking at the policeman. "Are you saying you can't do it?" he demanded. "Use your army, for God's sake. If it's too big a job for you to handle, we'll fly in troops from Germany to do it for you. And don't think we couldn't."

Harper smiled gently, as at some private joke, and the Ambassador looked uncomfortable. He was an old friend of the President's, and what he had heard had shocked him badly, but until a few months ago he had been a lawyer in the Midwest. Sometimes he still felt a little out of his depth in his new role. He was reluctant to slap down a CIA man whose only concern was safeguarding the President, but if this fellow Carpenter went any farther, he would have no alternative.

Wycliffe seemed to have sunk a little lower in his chair as, his big head cradled in his shoulders, he regarded Carpenter unwaveringly. "I have the greatest respect for the American army," he said flatly, "but I doubt very much if they could accomplish anything in two days in a strange city our own people can't."

"If your—" the CIA man began, flushing.

The Ambassador decided the time to intervene had come. "You haven't been in England very long, Mr. Carpenter," he observed firmly. "I guess our friends here understand that. Right now, it seems to me we need more practical suggestions. Do you agree, Peter?"

"I do," the Home Secretary said.

Wycliffe savoured Carpenter's expression.

"I guess everybody here knows that the Secret Service is responsible for the President's safety, sir," Harper remarked, looking at the Ambassador. "I'll be happy to go along with what Sir Brian has suggested, but I'd like to talk with him about those other steps he spoke of."

"Good," Wycliffe said.

FIFTEEN

As soon as the driver who took him home had gone, Lorimer phoned Melissa. When he told her he had had an accident and written off the Saab, she wanted to come round straightaway to make sure he was all right. Lorimer explained that really all he needed was sleep, and she agreed reluctantly to wait until the next morning. He hung up and went to bed.

Exhausted though he was, sleep didn't come quickly. When at last he dozed, it was only to wake after an hour and lie turning restlessly, his thoughts a jumble, until he dozed again. So it went on until eventually, in the early hours of the morning, he fell into a deep sleep from which he woke after eight o'clock feeling sluggish and unrefreshed. His head still ached, and large areas of his body felt as if a heavy lorry had been driven over them.

He made himself some coffee, took four more aspirin tablets, and looked out of the bedroom window. As far as he could see, nobody was watching the flat, and he wondered if Jenkins had satisfied the Shajihan, Ghanim, that there was nothing to be gained by continuing his surveillance.

Just before ten-thirty the doorbell rang and he went to answer it, expecting to find Melissa there. Instead it was the Welshman.

"How are you?" he asked.

"Not too bad," Lorimer told him. "Come in."

"It'd be better if we talked out here. That's why I didn't ring you." Jenkins looked round the landing. The door of Tiny's flat was closed, and there was nobody on the stairs.

"What do you mean?" Lorimer asked.

"Your flat may be bugged." Jenkins saw his incredulous expression. "To learn how much you know, and what you've told us. I've arranged for one of our people to have a look round."

"Thanks," Lorimer said ironically. "As long as it's not your friend Clive."

"It won't be. But why not him?"

"Melissa's coming round any time. She might scratch his eyes out. Have the police found anything yet?"

"No. We've heard from all the helicopter makers. The market's pretty depressed everywhere just now, and they haven't sold as many machines during the last four months as they would do in a normal year. Most of those they have went to the Services, big well-known firms, or finance companies."

"Our people won't have bought on h.p.," Lorimer said. "Why should they?"

"Use a false name, make one payment, then crash it and disappear," Jenkins suggested. "Helicopters don't come cheap."

"There'd be too many formalities, too many questions to answer. They wouldn't risk trouble for the sake of a few hundred thousand pounds."

"Maybe you're right. Every copper and traffic warden's being asked if they've seen a chopper where they wouldn't expect to, or anything that could be one on the ground." Jenkins was old enough to remember when the sight of a helicopter merely flying over was enough to make necks crane, now they were so commonplace nobody took any notice of them. "So far there's nothing."

Lorimer reflected that there were almost exactly forty-eight hours left, but he didn't say so. Jenkins was probably thinking the same.

Not long after the Welshman left, Melissa arrived looking lovely in fawn leather trousers and a thin cream-and-brown jumper. She kissed him as if she hadn't seen him for weeks, then stood back and regarded him critically.

"You don't look too bad," she said.

"It wasn't my face took the pounding," Lorimer told her.

"Oh. It was rotten luck. And your car, too."

Later, when they went out to lunch at a pub, Melissa tucked into a substantial meal while Lorimer picked at his food and spoke mostly in monosyllables. He wished he hadn't been at such pains to emphasize to Oldfield that the information he wanted was unimportant. He had done it to stifle any curiosity the manager might have felt, and it was true he had said he would like to know as soon as possible, but

Oldfield was unlikely to give it any priority. Most probably he wouldn't ring until late tomorrow afternoon, just before he left the office to go home. Or even the next morning.

Had the police found anything yet? It was twenty hours since they began their search, and time, their most precious asset, was slipping away.

Lorimer was no expert on explosives, but he hadn't needed Harper to tell him that a helicopter crashing in a crowded street would cause widespread damage and heavy casualties even if it wasn't loaded with explosives. If it was, there would be terrible devastation. The cars in the President's escort would be blown up, buildings might well be brought down, and hundreds of people trapped in them. Scores, possibly hundreds, would be killed.

"Are you all right, Gray?" Melissa asked, looking up from the generous portion of gateau she was steadily demolishing.

Lorimer dragged his thoughts back to her. "Yes, why?" he asked.

"You were miles away. You aren't taking any notice of me."

"I can't do anything else when I'm with you. I think of you all the time."

Melissa smiled, not in the least deceived. "Liar," she said pleasantly. "You've got something on your mind, but it isn't me. Oh well, as long as it's not another woman, I don't mind so much."

"It isn't," Lorimer assured her. Why couldn't he forget about terrorists and helicopters, leave them to Jenkins and the police for an hour or two, and just enjoy her company? he asked himself. It was a waste to think about other things when he was with her.

They drank their coffee, he paid the bill, and they went back to his flat.

At six-thirty, after Melissa had gone, he switched on the BBC television news. The main story was about diplomatic moves within the EEC; there was nothing about the President's visit or any threat to his safety. Lorimer hadn't expected there would be, and as soon as the news ended he turned the set off.

Not long afterwards Jenkins called. "I'm on my way home for an hour or two," he explained. "I have to be back on duty at twelve."

"Come in," Lorimer told him. "Will you have a drink?"

"Not now, thanks."

They went into the living room.

"Is it all right to talk?" Lorimer asked.

"Yes, you're clean now."

"Your man hasn't been yet."

Jenkins smiled. "He came while you were out."

"You mean he broke in?"

"That depends on what you mean by 'broke.' We didn't think you'd mind, as it was for your benefit, and I couldn't get him for long enough to come back again."

Lorimer wasn't sure whether he minded or not. There was something slightly unnerving about Jenkins' cool admission that his home wasn't inviolable, not only by burglars, but by the forces of law and order, too. Besides which, he hadn't taken the Welshman seriously when he suggested it might be bugged.

"Did he find one?" he asked with a hint of sarcasm.

"Four," Jenkins replied. "One of them was on the skirting board behind the head of your bed."

"The sods!"

The Welshman leaned back in his chair. Lines of weariness were etched into the skin of his face, and his tiredness showed in his eyes. Lorimer guessed he hadn't had much sleep during the last few days.

"We've only been able to trace two private individuals who've bought new machines for cash within the last four months," Jenkins said. "One was a builder and property developer in Yorkshire, the other was a man called Cummins who lives in Surrey. He's some sort of agent, and he has links with the Middle East; he acts for companies that trade out there. A twin-engined Bell 222 was delivered to his place three weeks ago."

"That sounds more like it," Lorimer commented. He told himself he mustn't be too relieved; this was only the start, they still had to find the helicopter. It might not even be the right one, he hadn't expected so big a machine. And why had it been delivered so long ago? "Is he straight?" he asked.

"As far as we can find out," Jenkins answered. "He hasn't a record, and the local police know nothing against him."

Which might mean nothing. On the other hand, there was no reason why Cummins shouldn't be straight, his knowledge of the business was probably limited to his receiving an order for a Bell 222 to be flown to somewhere in southern England. Quite possibly the order hadn't come from Shajiha. If he was honest, he would have done his best to establish that the helicopter wasn't destined for a country to which supplying them was illegal; if not, he wouldn't have done even that.

"What did he tell you?" Lorimer asked.

"Nothing. He's away. He operates from a small farm near Dorking, and nobody there knows where he's gone. His wife divorced him two or three years ago, and the implication was he's got a girl-friend somewhere, and he's with her. He isn't expected back until tomorrow night."

"Hell!"

"His secretary's on holiday, and the farm people don't have anything to do with his agency business. They saw the Bell land and take off again later the same day, but that's all they know. They've no idea where it is now." Jenkins hesitated. "There's one thing may help."

"What's that?" Anything was better than nothing, Lorimer thought.

"On that model the rotor blades don't fold, and they have a forty-six-foot span. It isn't the sort of machine you can tuck away in your garage."

That was something, Lorimer told himself, but it still left a multitude of possible hiding places: factories, warehouses, farms. Come to that, it wouldn't be difficult to camouflage a helicopter standing in the open. Disguise its shape with enough crates or bales, cover it with tarpaulins, and nobody would suspect what it was.

"It's there somewhere," he insisted. "It must be."

"They'll keep looking," Jenkins promised. "But I've a feeling they're not going to find it."

The words "if it exists" hung in the air between them.

Lorimer suspected Jenkins was right. He still believed that the helicopter was hidden somewhere in London or the Home Counties, but finding it was an immense task. It was a vast area. There must be tens of thousands of streets, thousands of factories and workshops, and hundreds of farms within its boundaries; how could they realistically hope to find the machine in the time they had left? It was less than forty hours now.

If they didn't find it, they would have to wait for it to show itself.

He had argued that that wouldn't be until Tuesday, and he still thought so, but what if he was wrong and the attack came tomorrow?

Jenkins was wishing he could be wholly convinced one way or the other: that Lorimer was right, or that he had dreamt up the whole thing. As it was, while he was prepared to go along with his theory, he still had reservations.

"Where will you be tomorrow?" he asked.

"At work," Lorimer answered. "Why?"

"I may need to get hold of you."

That was all.

"There's a Mr. Oldfield calling you from Dhartoum, Mr. Lorimer," the girl on the switchboard said.

Lorimer felt his nerves tense. He had been waiting for the call ever since he reached the office more than half an hour ago, but he hadn't really expected Oldfield to ring so early. It was still only just after nine-thirty. "Put him through, will you," he said.

"Hallo? Mr. Lorimer? You wanted me to ring you." Even over the phone, at a distance of nearly two thousand miles, Lorimer could hear that Oldfield had a cold.

"Yes," he agreed. "Just a minute." Crossing his room, he closed the door, causing Borrett, who had just come in, to look up and frown disapprovingly. "Were you able to find out anything?"

"Yes," Oldfield said. "The Carlton keeps records."

Lorimer felt like cheering. He made a note of what the manager told him, tore the top sheet off his pad, and stuffed it into his wallet. "Thanks very much," he said, "that should keep Accounts happy. There's another thing you may be able to tell me while you're on."

But Oldfield couldn't, and Lorimer had to wait two or three minutes while he went to find out. The answer, when it came, was less a surprise than it should have been. Lorimer thanked him, replaced the phone, and sat staring at it, wondering if he had said too much. It was hard to remember now just what he had said.

After a while he took down a book from the shelf over his desk and flipped through the pages until he found the entry he was looking for. It confirmed what he already suspected. Putting the book back, he went upstairs to Maxwells' offices.

As he stepped out of the lift, Forster emerged from his room.

Lorimer saw him hesitate, then, as if curiosity had overcome his reluctance, he walked towards him.

"Were you looking for me, Lorimer?" he asked.

"No."

"What are you doing here then?" Forster made no attempt to keep the dislike out of his tone.

"There are a few things I still have to see to just now."

For a second or two they faced each other, and Lorimer saw the animosity, amounting almost to hatred, in the older man's eyes.

"I don't like your hanging round Melissa," Forster said. "You aren't good enough for her."

Turning, he strode off. Lorimer stared after him. It was like a scene in a bad Victorian melodrama, he thought. Forster didn't worry him, but he was sorry for Melissa.

When he returned to his office ten minutes later, he found difficulty in concentrating on his normal work. Physically he still felt a good deal below par, and bits of his body ached spasmodically, but he knew it wasn't that. He was frustrated because he had no way of telling how far the police search had progressed, and whether they had found anything yet, and, most of all, because there was nothing he could do himself.

Despite his hint last night that he might, Jenkins hadn't rung by the time he left to go home. It probably meant the police still hadn't found anything and there was no news, Lorimer thought.

He got himself a scratch meal, and watched the Channel 4 news while he ate it. There were pictures of the American President and his wife arriving at Heathrow, but still nothing about any threat to his life. The *Financial Times* Thirty Share Index had risen by nearly four points, and the pound by three quarters of a cent against the dollar; a number of people had been airlifted to safety from the roof of a block of flats in west London when a fire, believed to have been caused by a gas leak in a kitchen, destroyed the top two floors; a man had been sent to gaol for life for murdering his ex-wife. Lorimer switched off.

He would have liked to go for a drink after he finished his meal, but decided to stay in in case Jenkins rang. There was nothing on television he felt like watching, he couldn't settle to reading a book he had started a fortnight ago, and when he tried to do the crossword in that morning's *Telegraph*, the clues made no sense to him. He knew the reason for his restlessness was that he was on edge and his mind was refusing to concentrate on anything, but the knowledge did nothing to help. He wasn't patient by nature; the waiting had lasted too long, and he was slightly punch-drunk. It wouldn't be much longer, he told himself; in a few hours it would be Tuesday morning.

That didn't help either. But at least nothing had happened today. It was past ten when the phone rang and he snatched it up.

"You weren't in bed, were you?" Jenkins asked.

"No." Suddenly Lorimer was alert. "What's happened? Have they found it?"

"No, Cummins is back. I've just seen him."

"What did he say?"

"He admitted right away he'd had an order for a Bell 222 and that it was delivered to his farm three weeks ago. He thought it was a bit strange the purchasers wanting it done that way, but he doesn't handle many planes and he didn't see any reason to query it. They completed the paperwork, told him they were attending to all the formalities, and took it out the same afternoon. He's no idea where they went."

"Nor who they were, I suppose?" Lorimer asked.

"No. He saw two men, an Arab who spoke good English and did all the talking, and the pilot. Cummins thinks he was Irish." Jenkins was using the phone in his car and the line crackled badly.

"What did you say?" Lorimer asked.

"Cummins thought the pilot who flew the chopper out was Irish. The order came from the Shajihan police; it was signed by your friend Inspector Mahfuz."

"He had to be involved. How did they pay?"

"A banker's draft on the National Bank of Shajiha in Gracechurch Street." Jenkins paused. "Two Shajihans flew in to Heathrow on Friday, a man and a girl. They weren't what they claimed to be, and if you're right about the Irishman, it could be one of them is going to fly the machine tomorrow."

"A girl?" Lorimer said.

"Yes. Remember Kipling. The Chief would like you to come in in the morning; is that all right?"

"Have I any choice?"

"You could roll your car down another hill and go to hospital," Jenkins suggested.

"What car?" Lorimer asked bitterly.

SIXTEEN

It was just after dawn, and the tower blocks of flats to the east were silhouetted against the lightening sky. Shajar, coming from her first prayers of the day, looked up and saw there was no cloud. Despite herself, she shivered. At home it would be much warmer than this, she thought, but here the sun seemed to have no strength, it was pallid like the skins of the people.

Shajar was a devout Muslim, and she always prayed diligently. These last few days, however, her prayers had possessed a new meaning and poignancy for her. It was as if she were seeing things she had never seen before. Then this morning she had suddenly realized that she would pray only once more before she died. It gave her a strange feeling to know with such certainty that something for which she had prayed all her life would soon be hers. It was that certainty, instilled in her from childhood by her mother and the ayatollahs, that enabled her to face today with so much joy and confidence.

She would like to have seen her mother and her younger brother and sister just once more, to say goodbye, but there had been no time, and perhaps it was better she should not see them. Last night she had written truthfully to her mother that she was happy and unafraid. Privately she hoped her mother would grieve a little for her, but she knew that behind her grief there would be a deeper joy and pride.

The last morning at Al Faktum they had told her what her task was to be, and said that she could decline it if she wished to, but that it was her last chance, and once she was in London it would be too late, because there would be no time to replace her. She had said at once she would go, proud that she had been chosen in preference to the two men with whom she had trained to strike this blow for her people. For Shajar, there were two enemies above all others: the Israelis, and the Americans who always supported them in everything. What she did today would echo round the world, compelling other nations to take notice and act at last to end the Zionists' aggression.

She knew that many people would die with her, but deaths were inevitable in war, and she was glad that some of them would be Americans; Americans had to die before their government would do anything. As for the British, they had been responsible for the idea of a new Israel, and now they were welcoming the American President.

Shajar looked round the asphalted yard. Until recently it had belonged to a firm of fruit-and-vegetable wholesalers, and to her right was the ramshackle corrugated-iron shed where they garaged their lorries. The lorries had gone, but the concrete floor was still stained with patches of oil, and some discarded tyres, worn to the canvas, were piled in an untidy heap in one corner. Behind her was the office block, its brickwork stained by rain-water and scarred by crumbling mortar. Part of the guttering hung down, and some panes in the windows were broken. For nearly four days that squalid, dilapidated building had been her home. When they first brought her here she had blushed at a picture of a nude girl on a calendar pinned to an office wall. One of the men had laughed at her embarrassment and been sharply rebuked by their leader, Abdul, who tore down the calendar and threw it away.

But it was to the building across the yard to her left she looked now, as if her eyes were drawn to it by some irresistible force. It was the old warehouse, a large, echoing cavern, part brick, part asbestos, and part corrugated iron. The front, which was in two wide sections, could be opened almost to the roof, nineteen feet above the ground, but now the great shuttered doors were closed, and the building was empty save for the helicopter squatting like some giant, slightly obscene insect in the middle of the floor. It was painted white, with tapering red-and-yellow stripes along the sides of its fuselage and a crest above them. Piled beside it on the floor were several stout boxes.

In everything except its paintwork the helicopter was identical with the one Shajar had flown in the desert, taking off and landing again and again, sending the sand rising in stinging, impenetrable clouds. Time after time she and the two men had practised approaching a convoy of three moving cars from the rear, hovering over the middle one, then dropping until the Bell was only a few feet above it and the sand swirling up obliterated everything. They had told her the helicopter had been acquired specially for their training. Now that training was over.

Her sadness at saying goodbye to her friends at the camp, particularly Ihsan, had been eased by her excitement at travelling to London and the prospect of the job she was to do. They had given her smart Western clothes in which she felt uncomfortable and self-conscious, and a special passport describing her as a diplomatic secretary. She had been a little afraid there might be difficulties when she arrived in England, but an official at Heathrow had actually smiled at her, and said he hoped she would enjoy her stay in Britain. If he had known why she was here, she thought, he wouldn't have smiled.

"Shajar!" a man called. She turned and saw Abdul standing in the doorway of the office block. "You must come so that we can film you."

He had explained to her last night about that. Not that any explanation had been necessary; she had seen the films of other young people who had done what she was about to do, some of them much younger than she was. Abdul had said that the tape they were going to make of her would be seen all over the world; she would be a heroine. That would be nice, she thought. It would make her mother and her brother and sister happy, but didn't they understand that she needed no such bribe?

She looked up at the sky again. The sun was high enough now for her to see it between two of the buildings. By the time it reached its zenith, her task would be done.

Slowly she followed Abdul indoors.

The four men looked up as Wycliffe walked into the room, his expression grim.

"A quarter of an hour ago a man with an Irish accent rang the *Mail*," he said. "He gave the IRA's code word and said that bombs timed to detonate at ten-thirty had been placed at the Bank of England, the Law Courts, the Imperial War Museum and the Tower."

Harper, the American, glanced at his watch. "It's ten-thirty now," he observed quietly. "Jesus! How do they expect anybody to clear an area and find a bomb in fifteen goddam minutes?"

"They don't," Cowper told him. "Maximum confusion, that's their aim." He paused. "If there are any bombs; it may be a hoax to distract attention from the real action."

"There are bombs," Wycliffe said in a flat tone. "The one at the Bank went off early, nearly ten minutes ago. It was left in an ambulance parked outside, and the police think there'll be a lot of casualties." He sat down in the vacant chair.

"Christ!" Cowper muttered. He wasn't prone to blasphemy as a rule.

"Does anything strike you about those four locations?" Wycliffe asked.

"They're all symbols of something?"

"I wasn't thinking of that." The Chief looked across at Lorimer, sitting at the end of the row.

"They're all well away from the President's route," the Scot said. He wondered if Wycliffe was suggesting that that invalidated his theory. He couldn't. In a way it strengthened it; you didn't launch diversionary attacks near the site of your main thrust.

"Yes." Wycliffe nodded and added grimly, "If you're right about the rest of it, it won't be long now."

Lorimer wasn't sure he wanted to be proved right. He knew that none of the other men there would blame him openly if he wasn't, they were professionals, and they would write off the search and all the rest of it as precautions they had had to take. The decisions and the responsibility were theirs. But they would remember the countless man-hours the search had involved, and the time of experts who could have been doing other work, and they wouldn't be human if they didn't blame him a little in their own minds. The next time they would remember, and the result might be disaster.

Jenkins was on the phone. He put it down now and said, "The Harriers are airborne."

"They've left it late enough," Harper muttered. "I hope to hell they know what they're doing."

No one answered him. Wycliffe and his men understood that if anything happened to the President today, it was the American Secret Service who would shoulder most of the blame. Some would attach to the British, but in their overheated search for scapegoats it was Harper and his colleagues the American media would crucify. They would allege that the Secret Service should have taken over the whole operation, and not trusted the President's safety to the Brits. That dozens, probably scores, of ordinary British people had been killed and injured merely because the President was a guest in their country would be incidental. Wycliffe, Cowper and Jenkins knew also that there was nothing to be gained by doing more than they had already done. If Lorimer was right, and all of them accepted now that he was, the quarry was a solitary helicopter whose target was known.

Put like that, it sounded easy.

The phone rang and the others watched intently as the Welshman walked over to answer it.

"*What?*" he exclaimed. "Yes, thanks very much. . . . You'll keep us advised? . . . Right. 'Bye." He replaced the phone on its rest. "That was the Yard. A copper at a station in the East End who'd been on leave for a couple of days came back on duty this morning. When he was asked about a helicopter, he said he'd seen one about three weeks ago. He couldn't be sure where it landed, but it was somewhere near a disused vegetable merchant's yard just off Redbourn Street. The Met are going in with the SAS."

"Now!" Cowper commented bitterly.

Nobody said what they were all thinking, that the police and the SAS would be too late. The President's car was due to leave Winfield House in five minutes, and there was nothing they could do now but wait. They sat, staring at the television screen on the table in front of them, each busy with his own thoughts. Apart from Lorimer, they were men trained to withstand pressure, and accustomed to it. They felt it now.

The double-glazing and thick curtains at the windows silenced the sounds of the traffic in the street five storeys below, and although more than a hundred people worked in the building, this small room seemed isolated.

Something haunted Lorimer. A memory. It was there, just beneath the surface of his conscious mind. Something he had seen or heard very recently. Something about the police. Suddenly it seemed desperately important he should remember.

Then it came to him, an item in the television news yesterday. There had been a bad fire at a block of flats. Some of the residents had taken refuge on the roof and . . .

He turned to Jenkins. "You said a helicopter would be spotted and chased away before it got near its target, didn't you?" he asked urgently.

"Let's hope I was right."

"There's one that wouldn't be."

They were all staring at Lorimer now.

"What's that?" Wycliffe demanded.

"A police chopper."

"The Met's Air Support Unit," Cowper said softly.

Wycliffe was frowning. "Are you saying you think one of their pilots could be involved?" he asked.

"No," Lorimer told him. "What machines do they fly?"

"God knows."

"Bell 222s," Cowper said.

"That's why they wanted the one they bought delivered three weeks ago; they needed time to paint it in the police colours."

"Oh no!" Cowper breathed.

"Right," Wycliffe said, getting to his feet. "Jenkins!"

He went out of the room, Jenkins at his heels, and the door closed behind them.

"If you're right . . . ." Harper remarked to Lorimer. He left the sentence unfinished.

Was he right? Lorimer wondered. It had been a shot in the dark, triggered by the memory of the television pictures of a police helicopter airlifting people to safety from the roof of the flats, and Jenkins' telling them that a constable in the East End had seen a helicopter three weeks ago. What were Wycliffe and Jenkins doing?

On the television screen three large black cars and their motor cycle escort were drawing away from the front of a large house. It was exactly twenty minutes to eleven. The three men left in the room leaned forward, gazing at the pictures as the procession turned out of the park. A policeman holding back a small crowd of sightseers saluted. There was a thin cheer, and some of the children waved little American flags. The man and woman in the back of the middle car smiled and waved back.

Lorimer thought irrelevantly that it was on days like this that London looked its best. The trees in the park were a brilliant green against the blue sky, their foliage not yet dulled by sun and dust, and people were strolling about in shirt-sleeves and summer dresses. But he knew the tranquillity was deceptive. Only a mile or two away a cloud of smoke and dust would be hanging like a pall over the City, marking another scene of terrorist death and destruction. And by now the other three bombs should have exploded. How many people had been killed and maimed this morning merely to divert attention from that sombrely gleaming car?

Shajar could no longer conceal it from herself: Strapped into her seat in the helicopter's cockpit, she was afraid. Closing her eyes, she told herself it was only a moment's weakness and would pass as quickly as it had come. What had she to fear? There would be no pain, nothing. In a single instant it would all be over. But it wasn't enough, and she couldn't bring herself to look at the crates fastened to the floor of the helicopter just behind her seat.

A few minutes ago they had wheeled the Bell out of the warehouse to the middle of the yard and started the engines. A few feet away Abdul was watching her anxiously. Was he afraid that even now she wouldn't be able to do it? He needn't worry.

Her watch said exactly ten forty-one. She raised her right hand, and saw Abdul nod. The roar of the Bell's engines rose to a crescendo, almost deafening in that confined space, and with a strange leisurely grace the helicopter lifted off.

Shajar could see the dust swirling in an angry cloud, and Abdul crouching, his hands half shielding his face, watching the Bell climb until it was above the level of the surrounding buildings. There was only a little dust, she thought. It was nothing like the whirlwinds of sand in the desert. She remembered them almost with affection as the helicopter continued to rise and she saw Abdul straighten up and go into the office building. Would he often think of her? she wondered.

She looked down on rows of derelict warehouses, the open spaces between them weed-grown and neglected. Many of the streets in this part of the East End were deserted, but along one of them a string of vehicles was driving eastwards, led by a white car with a flashing blue light. The police, Shajar thought. And those drab-green lorries, were they the army? Surely they couldn't have learned about the yard?

She flew over a busy street, and women doing their shopping looked up, surprised that a helicopter should be flying so low. Shajar had been taught at school that in England the sun rarely shone and much of the time it rained. Yesterday had been like that, dull with a thin mizzle of rain in the evening, and she had been afraid that the clouds would be so low today that she would be unable to see the car until she was only just above it. But this morning the only clouds were small puffs of white far to the north, and the sun glinted on the helicopter's newly painted fuselage. She picked up the line of the river and climbed higher.

A few seconds more and the Thames was below her, the sun dappling its murky surface with ripples of light. She could see it winding in great loops through the heart of the city, its succession of bridges stretching away into the far distance. For the last month of her training she had spent part of every day studying maps and pictures of this part of London. There were hundreds of photographs, taken on the ground and from the air, covering the whole area from Woolwich in the east to Chelsea in the west, all enlarged so that every building showed clearly, and now, although she had never been to Britain before, it was as if she were returning to a place she knew well. She felt a sense of triumph as she picked out landmarks she had memorized at Al Faktum, poring over the pictures in the concrete hut with the familiar desert all round. One of her instructors had been the Irishman, Sullivan.

She recognized the marina at St. Katherine's dock and checked her air speed. One hundred knots. There was no wind today, she must hold it at that. In the marina small boats were packed tight, while on the river other, bigger craft were moving slowly up- and down-stream, but as far as she could see in every direction, the sky was empty.

Two and a half minutes more. There was a cold vacuum inside Shajar and she felt numb. Suddenly her hands began to shake. She forced herself to concentrate on flying the helicopter, thinking carefully about every move she made, and picking out streets and buildings on the ground.

Tower Bridge passed below, and now she could see the old ships moored along the Embankment with, beyond them, the vast grey bulk of Somerset House. Her orders were to keep close to the south bank of the river as far as Hungerford Railway Bridge, and there to turn west along the line of Northumberland Avenue until she was over Trafalgar Square.

The President's car should reach the north end of Whitehall at exactly ten forty-eight. It was unlikely to be earlier, and if it should be a minute or two later, she must circle the immediate area and look out for it. No one would pay any attention to a police helicopter patrolling that part of London today. When she saw the car, she must descend to four hundred feet, wait until it was part of the way down Whitehall, then . . .

Thirty seconds to go. Shajar's hands were sweating, yet she felt cold. She told herself she must think of the car. Only of that.

Hungerford Bridge was just ahead and below her. To starboard she could see a tall monument she knew must be Nelson's Column, and there, about to enter the Square from the north, was a small procession of cars and motor cycles.

Shajar scanned the sky ahead and to each side of the helicopter. To the south-west and a good two thousand feet higher there was a tiny speck. It was too high for one of the real police Bells, she thought. More likely it was an air liner making for Heathrow.

Then she saw a second speck close to the first.

The Harrier pilots had already seen the helicopter. The leader put his plane into a flat dive, the other close behind.

Shajar saw them coming. During her training she had been told that there might be RAF planes on patrol, ready to see off any aircraft that strayed too close to that little convoy on the ground, and she told herself that when the pilots saw the helicopter's markings, they would turn away. She had to fly on, ignoring them. Then, by the time they realized anything was wrong, it would be too late.

The leading Harrier was close now, and although the pilot must have recognized the Bell's insignia, he wasn't flying off. Instead he was diving under the helicopter, so low that it seemed to Shajar he must crash into the river. Startled, she turned to watch as the Harrier came up on her starboard side, climbing and banking. The dive had been to impress her, she thought, he was going now, climbing to rejoin his companion.

She had almost forgotten the second plane, and with a sense of shock she saw that it was closing on her fast from port. At the last moment the pilot went into a steep turn. When he came out of it he was flying parallel with her only a few yards away, rocking his wings in a command to turn aside and land.

Shajar knew something was wrong. She was alarmed. In a few

seconds she would be over her target; nothing must be allowed to stop her. Gritting her teeth, she looked away.

Hungerford Bridge was immediately below her. She began her turn to starboard, and saw the little procession on the ground rounding the east side of the Square. Abdul's timing was perfect, she thought; when she turned again, along the line of Whitehall, the three cars would be just ahead of her. It reassured her that there were three, although she knew that it would have made no difference if there had been four or five; sufficient explosives were packed in the crate behind her to destroy a score of cars.

As she approached them from the rear, she must descend to fifty feet, come up to the middle one, and adjust her speed to theirs. She had rehearsed it so often, nothing could go wrong. She turned towards the other bank and the second Harrier climbed away.

On the ground people were gazing upwards. A small boy with his mother cried excitedly, "Mum! Mum, look! That Harrier's going to shoot down the helicopter."

"Don't be silly, Terry," his mother rebuked him. It was a stunt, she thought. Something for television.

Shajar, intent on picking out Northumberland Avenue, didn't see the first Harrier coming in on her port side, or know when its pilot fired. The Sidewinder air-to-air missile struck the Bell just behind her seat. Before the people on the ground heard the massive explosion, and felt its blast, the helicopter became a ball of fire.

The two fighters were climbing steeply, turning westwards.

"They're just flying off!" Terry's mother cried, aghast. She told herself it must all be part of the scene they were filming, and the helicopter was controlled by radio. They could do that, couldn't they? She looked round for a camera crew.

Around her, other people watched, shocked into silence, as the Bell disintegrated. The main section of its fuselage fell like a stone, burning, into the river, sending up a fountain of water. For several seconds afterwards smaller pieces followed, creating a succession of minor splashes. Even before the last of them had subsided, a launch pulled out from the pier and sped towards them, its bows raising a wave that fanned out and rolled back astern, spreading wider and flattening as it neared the bank. Where the helicopter had fallen the sun-dappled surface was smooth again.

On the Terrace of the House of Commons the Home Secretary waited until the sound of the Harriers' engines had faded into the distance, then he turned to the American Ambassador, who had been watching with him. "I'll tell the PM," he said quietly.

Together they turned and walked through the long corridors to where a knot of soberly dressed dignitaries were chatting while they waited for the President's car to arrive. They took little notice of the two men as they walked over to the Prime Minister and the Home Secretary murmured something. The Prime Minister nodded and half-smiled at the Ambassador.

At that moment the leading police motor cyclists entered the yard, and the talking stopped as the group watched the three Cadillacs drive in and the middle one come to a stop exactly level with the Prime Minister. The driver, as immaculate as his car, slid out of his seat and moved to the rear door. Before he could reach it, it was opened from the inside, and an elderly man in a dark suit, his black hair streaked with grey, got out.

There was a moment's puzzled silence. One or two of the party frowned. The Lord Chancellor, whose sight was not very good, glanced at the Speaker, and they took a step forward before stopping. The Prime Minister hadn't moved.

"That's not the President," somebody muttered in an affronted tone. "What the . . ."

The man who had got out of the car remained standing beside it uncertainly. The woman was still in her seat.

"That was Franklin," Cowper said, putting down the phone. "No other bombs have gone off, and the Yard don't think there are any; the IRA hoped to cause as much confusion as possible without running the risk of being caught planting them. The one at the Bank was intended to make us take their threat seriously."

"Any news about casualties?" Wycliffe asked.

"So far there are twelve dead and more than thirty injured."

"The bastards!" Harper said with quiet violence.

"The Harrier pilots reported it looked like a girl flying the helicopter," Cowper continued.

"The one who flew in on Friday," Jenkins said.

"Probably. The team that raided the yard in the East End found five men there. There was some shooting, and two of the men were killed. Two of the others and one of the SAS men were injured." Cowper paused. "One of the two who were injured was Kelly, the IRA explosives man who disappeared from Belfast a week ago."

"He was the link," Wycliffe commented. "That's just what they didn't want, to be tied in with the attempt to kill the President. Good."

Jenkins glanced at the screen. "The second car's just leaving," he said.

"Who was it in the first one?" Harper wanted to know. Now that the danger was over, the atmosphere in the room had changed, and his tone was almost casual.

"Two of our people," Wycliffe told him.

"Did they know?"

"Oh yes."

Lorimer's thoughts were on something else. "How did the Harriers know it wasn't a genuine police helicopter?" he inquired.

"There weren't any," Wycliffe answered with a grim half-smile. "When you produced your idea we just had time to get the Yard to call theirs down and see the Harrier pilots had orders to intercept any Bell 222 in that area and, if it wouldn't turn away and land, shoot it down."

SEVENTEEN

"From what I hear, you seem to have done a good job," Grantley said. "There'll be a lot of very grateful people here and in the States, I imagine. Now it's over."

"No," Lorimer told him.

"What do you mean?"

"It isn't over yet; there's still the person O'Brien phoned that night, the one who set up his murder."

The Chairman leaned back in his chair and regarded the younger man unwaveringly. "Do you know who it is?" he asked.

"Yes."

"Have you any evidence?"

"Enough to go to the police with. Hatem was waiting for me at the airport, so he must have known I was going out there. The people who run the camp were worried; Mahfuz had made sure that O'Brien's death was accepted as suicide, and scared Mrs. O'Brien badly enough to ensure she wouldn't cause trouble, but I might ask a lot of awkward questions. Once the body was back in England, I could even demand an inquest."

Grantley said nothing. He knew that if Lorimer had had his way, there would have been an inquest, and the course of events might have been different, but he wasn't a man to look back over his shoulder when doing so would achieve nothing.

"Whoever told them I was coming had to be in London," Lorimer went on. "The local office didn't know until the next morning; I checked the telex. It struck me as odd nobody had let Oldfield know earlier, but they didn't want him meeting me at the airport."

"I gave instructions for him to be told as soon as I'd decided who was going," the Chairman said.

"Did you?" Lorimer's voice was flat. "The only people who knew were Rayment, Forster, your secretaries, my wife and Forster's daughter."

"And me," Grantley said.

Their eyes met.

"And you," Lorimer agreed. "There were two or three people at the Shajihan Embassy, I had to get a visa, but I was fairly sure the message came from here. I reckoned I could rule out my wife and Melissa Forster and the three secretaries. That left Rayment, Forster —and you.

"Mrs. O'Brien told me that, apart from one or two local calls, the one her husband made when he got back the night before he was killed was the only one either of them made from the hotel. She was sure about it. Yet there was a charge of over ten pounds for phone calls on their bill. When I rang Oldfield he found that the Carlton keeps records of outgoing long-distance calls, they go through their switchboard, and they gave him the number O'Brien rang."

"That's not proof," the Chairman said roughly.

Lorimer took out his wallet, and from it extracted the list Oldfield had prepared for him. "Put that with it," he said.

Grantley took the list and studied it. "What are these dates?" he asked.

"The dates of the *Maxwell Pride*'s sailings from Dhartoum during O'Brien's visits," Lorimer told him. "Except the first, that was a mistake."

"How?"

"It's before O'Brien was appointed Overseas Manager. When I asked Oldfield to let me have the dates he couldn't remember when O'Brien took over, and he went back too far. Lyddon didn't know how long the *Maxwell Pride* had been taking on extra hands at Dhartoum because he only joined her three years ago, so when Oldfield rang me back about the phone call, I asked him. It had been going on for nearly four years, and the Overseas Manager from London always arranged it."

"My God!" Grantley muttered. "Forster!"

"Yes," Lorimer agreed. "O'Brien didn't start it, he just carried on. He believed what Forster told him, that the men were escaped political prisoners. After I'd talked to Oldfield I went to look at the *Maxwell Pride*'s logs. All the other ships' were there, but hers had been removed. Forster must have done it after I told you about the extra hands on Saturday. I said then that O'Brien had lived too well for a man on his salary; the same's true of Forster when you remember he's only been a director of Maxwells for a couple of years, and that before then he wasn't earning any more than Oldfield. Yet three years ago he could afford to buy that flat in Chelsea." Lorimer paused. "The other evening Melissa and I went out to dinner at a little Italian restaurant. Nobody there knew us, and we didn't see anybody we knew, but the next morning Forster said something to her about her being out with me. Somebody must have followed us and told him; probably one of the men he had search my flat to see if I had anything there that might incriminate him.

"On Saturday I told you both I was waiting for Oldfield to ring me back. That scared him. He had to make sure I didn't get the call, so he told you he had to get back for an appointment, waited around until he saw me leave, then followed me. You know where the road goes round the top of that big valley?" Grantley nodded. "He cut me off up there, and forced me off the road. I went down the hill and my car was a write-off; it blew up."

"My God!" Grantley said again. "Have you told the police or your friend Jenkins about him?"

"Not yet."

"Why haven't you?"

"There hasn't been a lot of time. I had to wait to see what happened this morning because, if I was wrong about that, nobody would take me seriously about Forster. It didn't matter waiting, it was too late for him to do anything; the Arabs and the IRA would have gone ahead whatever he told them."

Grantley sat quite still, his hands resting on his desk. "How well do you know his daughter?" he inquired.

"Pretty well."

"All right, leave it to me. I'll do what has to be done."

The Chairman wouldn't be able to keep United's name out of the papers now, Lorimer thought. He walked to the door. He had been ready to go to the police, but he was glad Grantley had said he would do it instead.

Grantley waited until Lorimer had closed the door behind him, then, his expression grim, he picked up one of the phones on his desk.

Lorimer slept badly that night. When he was awake he thought about Melissa. She had told him she was going away for a couple of days and wouldn't be back until late that night. Unless the police contacted her, the first she knew about her father's arrest would be when she saw the papers tomorrow. Poor Melissa.

In the morning, although he still ached, he felt better than he had done since Saturday afternoon. He washed, shaved, dressed and went to work as usual. On the tube he read his *Telegraph*. On the front page there was a long report of the bomb explosion outside the Bank of England, the latest casualty figures were nineteen dead and forty injured, but he could find nothing about Forster. Nor was there anything about the attempt on the President's life. Then, near the bottom of an inside page, he came across a two-paragraph story about the RAF testing new equipment the previous day. Repelling a mock attack on the Houses of Parliament, a Harrier using the equipment had shot down a radio-controlled target helicopter. So that was how they were playing it, he thought.

At twenty past ten, Mrs. Wilkins rang down to tell him that Sir Aidan would like to see him right away. Wondering why the Chairman should want to see him again, Lorimer put on his jacket and walked along the corridor to the lift.

As he passed his door, Borrett looked up and called, "Are you going out?" He disliked not knowing his PA's whereabouts and what he was doing.

"The Chairman wants me," Lorimer told him. He despised Borrett. Now all this was over, he would start looking seriously for another job.

The lift took him up to the top floor.

"He wants you to go straight in," Helen Wilkins said, standing up and smiling. She walked across to the door of the Chairman's room, opened it, and announced, "Mr. Lorimer, Sir Aidan." Just as she had done a fortnight ago, Lorimer thought.

Grantley was sitting at his desk. "Sit down, Lorimer," he said.

Lorimer obeyed.

For nearly a quarter of a minute the Chairman gazed at him in silence, but his eyes were blank and it was clear that his thoughts were somewhere else.

"I thought I should tell you at once," he said at last. "I heard a quarter of an hour ago; Forster gassed himself in his car last night."

Lorimer's first reaction was shock. It hadn't occurred to him that Forster might take that way out. Then he remembered that Grantley had said he did it "last night," and he realized what must have happened. The sense of shock hardened into anger.

"You warned him," he said bitterly.

Grantley met his gaze, and there was anger in his eyes, too. He hadn't known Forster well, and he hadn't particularly liked him, but now he had to accept part of the responsibility for what Maxwells' Managing Director had done, as well as what he himself, deliberately, and knowing what the consequences would be, had done yesterday after Lorimer left him. He could live with the knowledge, but he would never forget.

"I didn't warn him," he said harshly. "I told him. What would happen."

"Why?"

"Because I decided it was the best thing to do. Not necessarily the right thing, but the best. What good would it have done for him to stand trial and go to gaol? It would have cost the taxpayer a small fortune. For what? So that people could read about it in their papers, and feed their self-righteous little souls? The Government wouldn't have wanted a trial: In another few years those extremists may be in power in Shajiha, and if they are, we shall have to deal with them. United's name would have been dragged in the mud all over the world. You think it's an organization in itself, almost like a small state. It isn't; it's tens of thousands of small shareholders and people whose pensions and insurance premiums are invested in it. Trade unions, charities. And it's a hundred thousand employees in fifty different countries. My job is to do the best I can for them, all of them, not for some abstract concept of truth."

"He had O'Brien murdered," Lorimer said bitterly. "And he tried to kill me. He was a crook, he hadn't even a cause. All he cared about was lining his own pockets, and he didn't mind where the money came from, or how many people were killed, so long as he got it."

"You think he hasn't paid?" Grantley demanded. More quietly he added, "He said he didn't know about the terrorists in Europe."

"You mean he didn't mind helping them provided they didn't operate too near home," Lorimer said with contempt. "Anyway, he was lying. Where did he think the men he smuggled out to Italy and Spain were going to set off their bombs, or shoot people they didn't agree with? Hadn't the people who've been maimed for life, and the widows and orphans a right to see him tried?"

"What about his daughter?" Grantley asked roughly. "Would you want her to live through it all? Facing the Press and all the publicity, visiting him in gaol for the next twenty years?"

Would he? Lorimer thought. Damn Grantley! "Who found him?" he asked.

"A neighbour who has the next garage." Grantley shifted in his chair, and when he spoke again it was more mildly. "Stop expecting life to be all fine and beautiful; it isn't, and you're too old for that sort of sloppy idealism." Standing up, he walked over to the nearer of the big windows and looked out. "You won't be going back to your job," he said over his shoulder. "It's redundant; Gerald Borrett doesn't need a PA. I'm making a new appointment, a sort of trouble-shooter to be attached to my office and work directly for me. Do you want the job?"

"Me?" Lorimer was startled.

"They told me you were an uncouth Scot." Grantley turned. "You're an uncivilized bloody race, you know that? You boast there's nobody like you, and you drink toasts to a mixture of offal and oatmeal. My God!"

Lorimer grinned. "There used to be a sign at the Border," he said. "Going north it read 'Welcome to Scotland.' Coming south it was 'Beware of the sheep.'"

Grantley regarded him thoughtfully. "Do you want the job?" he demanded.

* * *

Lorimer was weary. Unusually for him, he felt lethargic; he couldn't even be bothered to get himself a meal. Tomorrow he would be back to normal, but for the moment all he wanted was to relax and forget everything that had happened. After that there would be the new job to look forward to. The phone rang and Lorimer went to answer it. It was Melissa.

"You bastard, Gray," she said. She was crying. "It was your fault Dad killed himself, you made him. He said in his letter you'd managed to dig up something he'd done. God, how I hate you!"

"Look—" Lorimer began. But Melissa had replaced her phone.

About the Author

Ian Stuart is a successful writer living in England. He is the author of twelve previous mystery novels, including *Pictures in the Dark* and *The Garb of Truth*.